THE PROTECTOR
and the
Generation Before

By Jennifer M Beagon
Edited by Shannon McGee
Illustrated by Áine Beagon

This book is a work of fantasy fiction by Jennifer M. Begaon

ISBN: 9798446157754

Imprint: Independently Published

ACKNOWLEDGMENTS

So, here it is, my third and final book in the Protector trilogy! What an experience it has been, from starting the first book in 2014, to years of wanting it published but at the same time being too mortified to let anyone read it, and finally, just taking the bull by the horns one day and self-publishing it, I haven't looked back. The feedback from the first two books has been amazing and heart-warming, encouraging me to get on to write the third and final book in this trilogy.

As always, I want to thank my husband and our two girls for both believing in me and encouraging me as well as allowing me the time to write, which often meant eleven- or twelve-hour days of me in front of the laptop.

A special mention also to my Mam and Dad for their constant love, support, and encouragement. To see how proud they were of me when they seen my first book in print was a wonderful moment.

I must thank my lovely Editor, Shannon McGee, for editing this book for me, having the book professionally edited has perfected it in a way I could not. Also, just to thank Shannon for her encouragement and support.

A little mention to a fantasy fiction loving girl called Ruby, who was the very first person to buy and read The Protector and the Legend of the Swans and has since become The Protectors biggest fan! Thank you, Ruby, for loving the books and for all the readers who have sent me so many lovely messages. Each message I receive about the books means the absolute world to me, so please keep them coming!

I would also like to thank my friend Mark Eagers, who designed and handmade the beautiful Fairy Door on the front cover of this book, it's just as I imagine the door to An Crann Darach Sean would look.

To my daughters, Áine for her beautiful and talented illustrations and to Eimear for her patience in listening to me read aloud sections of the story.

Lastly, I would just like to say that although this is the end of The Protector trilogy, I think the ending has opened the door for a new series of stories, so watch this space!

I hope you enjoy this book!

CHAPTER 1:

It was a Saturday evening, Fidelma was sitting on the edge of her bed with her phone in her hand and one of her legs bouncing up and down as she waited impatiently for Fairy Áine to arrive. Fidelma was feeling a mixture of emotions, shock at the revelation that the man in the photo was not only her Grandad but also Mon, King of the Merrows! Sorrow that everyone in her family presumed he was dead when in fact he was living it up in his Kingdom. Annoyance that once again Fairy Áine had kept a huge secret from her, and apprehension about the implications of this latest bombshell.

After a half hour of waiting, Fidelma took a deep breath as she watched the lid of the treasure chest open and Fairy Áine popped out. When she finally settled on Fidelma's lap she frowned with her hands placed on her hips as she spoke, "Fidelma mo chara, what is the matter?"

Fidelma scowled as she unlocked her phone and opened the photos app. "Guess who I seen a photograph of today Fairy Áine, my dear friend?" she asked scathingly.

Fairy Áine shook her head nervously, she could tell Fidelma was annoyed but she had no idea why. It was completely out of character. Fidelma turned her phone around to Fairy Áine to show her the photo that she had taken. It was the picture her Auntie Mary had shown her earlier. Fairy Áine stared at the phone in awe.

"Oh Fidelma," she cried as she flew up in front of Fidelma's face and touched her cheek gently with her hand.

Fidelma pulled away abruptly. "How could you Fairy Áine? How could you lie to me again? And did you lie to my Granny too? How could you all let her think her husband was dead? I can't believe I trusted you, any of you!" Fidelma said bitterly to a hurt Fairy Áine. She jumped up from the bed and walked over towards the window where she stared out at the rain, her hands shaking as she wiped at the tears now streaming down her face.

"Fidelma," Fairy Áine started gently, "I did not lie to your Granny, she knew where King Mon was, she visited him regularly, and it was your Granny Fidelma who made me promise not to tell you until you were eighteen, she thought it would be too much for you to take in."

Fairy Áine flew over to Fidelma and smiled wryly as she extended her tiny hand "If you come with me, I will explain everything."

CHAPTER 2:

1937

Fidelma was walking home from the local grocery shop where she worked five days a week, it was only a fifteen-minute walk from her home and she enjoyed working there. She served the same people most days, local people from the village where she lived with her parents and siblings. A few weeks ago, Fidelma's sister Nora had start working at the shop too, she took over Fidelma's previous duties of sweeping and mopping the floor every day and washing out the glass bottles and jars that the customers returned to the shop daily. Fidelma now worked the counter where she served the customers. Both girls were walking home together now, tired from another busy day but grateful to have work as they knew plenty of girls their age were not as lucky, and some were rumoured to be heading to England.

Ryan's Groceries and Dried Goods was the main shop in the village. The shop was owned by Michael Ryan, brother of Peter Ryan – who was, Fidelma's father. Fidelma and her family lived on a small farm at the edge of the village where Peter Ryan had some cows and hens. With the cows, he supplied his brother's grocery shop with milk, butter, and cheese while his wife Mary tended to the hens who supplied the eggs for the grocery shop. The shop was a family business that provided well enough for them, and meant that all their children would have work and not have to emigrate like so many others.

When the girls got home, they helped their mother with some household chores before they set the table for supper. In the evening when the three younger children, Brian, Sean, and Nellie had gone to bed, Nuala and Nora sat by the fire knitting, this was when Fidelma went out for her walk. Every evening she climbed over the wooden gate at the back of their house and walked down the small path that led to the end of the field where the cows were kept. There stood a tall oak tree, its branches seeming to spread out like arms protecting the farm. Sitting on the lowest branch of the tree was Fairy Áine as she waited patiently for Fidelma, her friend and Protector.

1938

Fidelma was sitting at the table in the kitchen of An Crann Darach Sean and she was absolutely distraught. Fairies Áine, Eimear and Caoimhe were trying desperately to console her, but their efforts were proving futile.

Earlier that day Fidelma had witnessed the petrification of her beloved youngest sister Nellie while she and her family were having a picnic. And so Fidelma and her family had spent the day with the Guards (the Irish police). Fidelma felt terrible that there was a man hunt for her sister, when here she was sitting on the table in front of her, having been turned into stone by the evil Balor.

Fairy Áine had tried unsuccessfully to use a spell to save little Nellie, but Balors magic proved too strong. As it turned out, the only way to free little Nellie was to kill Balor, however he had disappeared back beneath the earth and would not appear again for another seventy-eight years as Fidelma's granddaughter would find out.

Holding Fidelma's hand, Fairy Áine spoke. "Fairy Eimear, will you make some lavender tea please? it might help to settle her some."

Fidelma turned to look at Fairy Áine, her eyes raw and her cheeks red and soaked from crying. "What am I going to do Fairy Áine?", she cried beseechingly to her friend, "how can I face my parents? My family? This is all my fault! Please, please can I just stay here so

I don't have to face them?" she pleaded as she collapsed into fresh tears.

The fairies exchanged sorrowful looks, they felt Fidelma's pain and as much as they wanted to, they knew they could not take it away. Fairy Eimear covered her face with her hands as she felt the tears spring to her eyes. Fairy Caoimhe tilted her head back and blinked repeatedly in an attempt to stop the tears that were threatening to stream down her face.

Fairy Áine bit her lip as she stroked Fidelma's hair "Now you listen to me Fidelma Ryan," she began firmly, "None of this is your fault, the only person to blame here is Balor and I promise you some day we will save little Nellie, I don't know when but believe me, it will happen."

Fidelma turned her tear-stained face towards Fairy Áine. "Do you really think so?" She begged.

Fairy Áine nodded. "I know so, but until then, I need you to be brave and strong, you cannot let Balor win. His day will come, it could be in the next few weeks or Fidelma it could be in fifty years!"

Fidelma gasped despairingly at this, but Fairy Áine continued.

"Fidelma, little Nellie is not dead, she has been stopped, frozen in time, she will get to live her life, just not now, and…when we do eventually save her, she will begin a new life, but you need to live *your* life now Fidelma, you cannot give up. Your parents need you; your brothers and sisters need you; we need you."

Fidelma sniffled and wiped her cheeks with the back of her hand before leaning into Fairy Áine for a hug. Fairies Eimear and Caoimhe looked on as the two friends held each other tight.

1939

At the beginning of this year Peter Ryan had done a deal that would see the family move out of their home and into a smaller, more modern house up the back of the field. A new road was being built through their village that required the land where their house and best part of their farm sat, this also meant having to give up the farm, but Peter Ryan was paid handsomely for the deal and they could still keep the hens. The family now had a new home with a large back garden which Peter Ryan split in two and used one half for growing vegetables which he sold to his brothers shop.

This came at an ideal time for the Ryan family as the world was on the brink of war and everyone was feeling anxious. As a treat, Peter Ryan decided to take his family to visit his parents in Co. Kerry, things were quiet at the grocery shop where the girls worked, so their uncle agreed to give them the summer off, he felt they deserved it too after all the family had been through in the past year. It was was agreed that they would set off on Monday morning, they were getting the train and there was great excitement in the house for the first time since the disappearance of little Nellie. The Sunday evening before they were due to leave, Fidelma walked out to the back garden, down to the oak tree and waited for Fairy Áine to appear.

Fairy Áine took Fidelma into An Crann Darach Sean where she was greeted warmly by the other fairies. They sat down at the table where fairies Eimear and Caoimhe were setting tea, brown bread, butter, and jam.

Fairy Áine took a sip from her tea. "So tell me Fidelma, what is this dilemma you have?"

"Well," began Fidelma, "Daddy is taking us all on a holiday to visit my grandparents, he says he will stay for a week or two but then he and Mammy will return home and me and my brothers and sisters will stay for the rest of the summer!"

"Oh" Fairy Áine beamed, "sure that sounds wonderful Fidelma, aren't you glad?"

"Well, I am looking forward to it, and to seeing my grandparents, but how will you come to me Fairy Áine? You've always appeared at the oak tree!"

Fairy Áine smiled. "Oh Fidelma, there are always other ways, I am sure we can come up with something, let me see, where exactly are you going? Where do your grandparents live?"

"In Co. Kerry," answered Fidelma, "near the three lakes!"

The three fairies looked at each other and smiled knowingly. Fairy Áine patted Fidelma's hand. "Well, that is perfect Fidelma, we have some friends who live there so leave it with me."

Fairy Áine

CHAPTER 3:

It was Monday evening and the Ryan family had just arrived at their destination in Co. Kerry. Granny and Grandad Ryan lived in an old farmhouse near the three main lakes in Killarney, although they were tillage farmers, they had reduced their crop in recent years as they were getting on in age. Their youngest son Patrick however still lived with them and worked on the farm. The children loved it here, it had been a couple of years since their last visit so there were emotional scenes in the old farmhouse. Granny Ryan kept wiping the tears from her eyes with the old apron that she wore. Of course, the conversation quickly moved to the disappearance of little Nellie and Fidelma's father explained how he had let the local Gardaí back in Co. Dublin know where they were heading should any news arise on little Nellie, and his brother Patrick told him he would take him down to the local Gardaí barracks first thing in the morning. Fidelma was feeling fraught with anxiety at the mention of little Nellie, and she wished she had access to the oak tree at the back of her garden so she could see Fairy Áine. She wondered now what Fairy Áine had in mind for visiting Fidelma while she was in Co. Kerry, for she was very secretive about it, just telling Fidelma it would be a lovely surprise for her.

There were two big old beds in one of the bedrooms upstairs, the children all squeezed into one and Fidelma's parents slept in the other one, everyone fell asleep straight away that evening after their long day travelling.

The following morning Fidelma's mother was helping Granny Ryan to dish out porridge to everyone as Fidelma and Nora set the table and made the tea. "What are ye going to get up to today then?" Grandad Ryan asked the children. Nora looked at her father, "Well I thought I could take a lift with Daddy and go for a walk about the village?"

"I don't see why not." Peter Ryan replied, "It's your Uncle Patricks cart though so you may ask him."

Nora looked shyly to her Uncle Patrick who merely winked. "I'll take ye Nora."

Everyone turned to look at Fidelma then, so she spoke up too, "Well I was thinking I might take a walk down to the lakes, it's such a beautiful morning."

Grandad Ryan nodded. "Do Fidelma, do."

When breakfast was finished Nora headed off with her father and Uncle Patrick while Fidelma helped clean up. Granny Ryan came over and rubbed the back of her coarse hand against Fidelma's cheek, "You're a grand girl Fidelma so ye are." She said to her Granddaughter, "go you off now and enjoy your walk down to the lakes, 'tis very peaceful around there."

Fidelma put her arms around her Granny and hugged her tight. "Thanks Granny," she said before turning to her mother, "I'll take the younger ones out for a walk when I get back." And she set off on her walk.

The sky was blue with just a scattering of fine clouds, the type that you can almost see through, they reminded Fidelma of the cobwebs on the ceiling in her old school. The walk to the lakes was not too far from the Ryan's farmhouse and Fidelma was amazed at how quiet it was apart from the squawking of some seagulls.

As Fidelma approached the main and largest of the three lakes, Lough Leane, she took off her shoes and stockings as she tread carefully over the stones and rocks at the water's edge, the clear water gently lapping over her feet, soothing them after her walk.

Fidelma bent down to pick up a flat stone so she could skim it across the lake as her father had taught her, but when she stood up again something caught the corner of her eye, and she had the unsettling feeling of being watched. Fidelma turned to her right, the sun was blinding so she had to shade her eyes with her hand to see more clearly, however she was relieved to see a young girl sitting on the rocks with her legs resting in the water. The girl lifted her arm and gave Fidelma a friendly wave, so Fidelma smiled and waved back as she navigated her way over the stones and rocks towards the girl.

"Hello!" Fidelma called as she got close to the girl, she noticed the girl seemed to be wearing a revealing swimming costume, Fidelma thought she must be an American tourist.

"Hello there!" the girl called back. Fidelma noted the girl had hair so blonde it was almost white, and it fell in big loose curls all the way down her back and was resting on the rock she sat on. Fidelma raised her eyebrows as she admired it. "You have the most beautiful hair I have ever seen!" she exclaimed.

"Thank you so much Fidelma." The girl smiled with a cheeky grin.

That stopped Fidelma in her tracks. "How do you know my name?"

The girl giggled. "Sorry my name is Meara, I am a good friend of Fairy Áine's, I have been waiting for you!"

Fidelma was stunned. "You know Fairy Áine? Are you a Protector too?"

The girl giggled again. "Oh no, no Fidelma, I am not a Protector, sure that is your job."

Fidelma was confused, she thought she was the only one who

Fairy Áine appeared to in their world, if she was honest, it made her feel special,and she was unsure how she felt to find out that she was not the only one. "What are you then?" she asked the girl.

The girl with the white, blonde hair smiled and tilted her head to the side as she replied, smiling. "Why, I am a mermaid Fidelma!" And with that she lifted her massive mermaid tale from the water where Fidelma thought her legs were and flapped it about before bringing it back down to the water with a splash.

Fidelma wiped the water that had splashed over her from her face as she stared at the girl in front of her, speechless. She watched wide eyed as the girl, Meara, gently this time, lifted her tail from the water and turned to settle it on the rocks beside her. The tail had thousands of tiny golden coloured scales which glittered and shimmered beneath the sunlight.

Meara smiled at Fidelma as she patted a rock beside her. "Come cailín, come and sit beside me."

Fidelma looked at the girl for a moment, then she looked around her at the lakes and rocks, they were alone, so she nodded and carefully made her way towards the rock that Meara had offered her as a seat.

Once Fidelma was safely seated Meara put out her hand. "Very pleased to meet you Fidelma."

Fidelma took the mermaids hand, still in shock, and shook it gently. "Pleased to meet you too." She replied.

"So," said Fidelma, unsure what to say "You're a mermaid! I didn't think mermaids were real!"

"Actually-" replied Meara, "I am a merrow, I suppose some people might call us mermaids but in old Ireland we are merrows - and *yes*, Fidelma we are very real, as real as the fairies who have become your friends."

Fidelma felt her cheeks redden slightly at this, of course she knew now that anything was possible but she never in her wildest dreams imagined that mermaids were real.

"Are there many of you?" Fidelma asked.

"Oh yes!" replied the beautiful Meara. "I live in the Kingdom of Leane where my father and mother are the King and Queen of the merrows."

Fidelma stared at the figure sitting beside her, mouth agape and speechless.

Meara giggled again. "Don't look so surprised Fidelma, you have been to An Crann Darach Sean, and you have battled against the evil Balor have you not?"

Fidelma simply nodded.

"So then why the wonder? I would have thought you would be used to such creatures by now."

Fidelma smiled and shook her head. "So did I, but you are definitely the biggest surprise. Did Fairy Áine give you a message for me?"

"Oh!" Meara gasped, her hand flying to her mouth "How silly of me, I almost forgot!" She reached behind her to produce a small wooden treasure chest which she handed to Fidelma.

Fidelma took the chest gingerly from Meara. It was made from a dark shiny wood with intricate Celtic carvings and a brass latch with a little keyhole, she ran her fingers over the markings in wonder. "Is this a real pirates' chest?"

"It is Fidelma, but it belongs to you now."

Fidelma looked up suddenly. "What? How do you mean? What am I to do with it?"

"Well," smiled Meara "You are to keep it in your bedroom I suppose, Fairy Áine said to tell you to keep it locked until the sun starts to set and then you can unlock it."

"And then what?" asked Fidelma feeling apprehensive all of a sudden.

"And then…" smiled Meara, "- you'll see!"

Fidelma stared at Meara, then at the chest and back at Meara again. "What if the pirates want it back?"

Meara giggled. "Oh Fidelma come along now, you surely are not afraid of some pirates are you?" before waiting for Fidelma to answer though, she continued, "I promise you do not need to worry yourself about pirates, this is a gift, from your friend Fairy Áine - and, if you are going to be here for a while…then I was hoping I could be your friend too."

Fidelma looked at the beautiful Meara who suddenly looked vulnerable as she waited for Fidelma to answer. Fidelma smiled. "I would love to be your friend Meara."

Meara smiled a big toothy grin, swung her tail around back into the water with a splash and dived into the lake, disappearing beneath the still water for a moment. Fidelma stood up on the rock she had been sitting on and waited for Meara to reappear, her eyes searching the lake, when suddenly, the white, blonde hair of her new friend appeared and her head gracefully broke through the stillness of the water. Fidelma smiled and clapped her hands in delight.

"Will you come back tomorrow my friend?" Meara asked.

Fidelma nodded enthusiastically. "Yes of course."

Fidelma put her hand up to wave off her new friend when a thought suddenly occurred to her. "Wait!" she called, "Meara! Wait! You didn't give me a key!"

"Lift the latch." Meara called, nodding towards the chest in Fidelma's arms.

Meara waved before disappearing beneath the lake again, Fidelma ran down the rocks to the edge of the water to see if she could see her, but Meara was gone.

Fidelma sat down again and carefully lifted the latch on the chest, she opened the lid slowly. The inside of the chest was covered in a deep red cloth and sitting there on its own inside the chest was a tiny key. Fidelma lifted the key out and thought about where she could put it to keep it safe when she remembered the charm bracelet her beloved grandmother had given to her when she had turned 16, it had a tiny fairy charm on it. Fidelma's granny had given it to her as a gift for her birthday just as she revealed her other gift, that of the Protector, her granny had passed away shortly afterwards so Fidelma treasured the charm bracelet. She carefully attached the tiny key to it and knew it would be safe there always.

CHAPTER 4:

Fidelma and her family were having supper around the kitchen table that evening. Grandad Ryan was standing at the head of the table slicing through a freshly baked loaf of bread while Granny Ryan brought a slab of butter and a jar of homemade blackberry jam to the table. Fidelma's mother was organising the tea; the kitchen was busy with chatter and Fidelma thought her parents looked relaxed for the first time since little Nellie 'disappeared'.

"Did you go down to the lakes Fidelma?" her Grandad asked as he put a thick slice of bread on her plate.

"I did Grandad." Fidelma replied, "It was lovely and peaceful; I think I will go down every morning for a walk."

"That you should Fidelma, that you should." Her Grandad replied as he took a sip of his tea.

The sun was beginning to set so Fidelma had gone up to the bedroom before the younger ones were sent to bed. She sat with the treasure chest on her lap for a few minutes wondering if anything at all was going to happen when a rattling sound inside the chest made her jump. Fidelma stood up quickly and sat the chest down on the bed, she took a step back and watched the chest as it rattled when all of a sudden, the lid popped open and a tiny ball of light shot up out of it and bounced around the room until it finally came to a stop on the bed and revealed itself to be none other than Fairy Áine. "Phew!" she exclaimed, "That was fun!" and she gave a little giggle.

Fidelma laughed, she was both relieved and astonished to see the little fairy."Oh Fairy Áine, it is so good to see you."

Fairy Áine smiled and extended her tiny hand. "Let's go!"

Fidelma took the fairy's hand and in a flash of light she was transported to the entrance of An Crann Darach Sean where Fairy Áine made her fairy size so they could enter. Once inside Fairy Eimear greeted Fidelma warmly with a hug. "How are you Fidelma? How are you and your family enjoying your trip to County Kerry?"

Fidelma hugged Fairy Eimear back."Oh it is just lovely Fairy Eimear, we are having a lovely time, it is so good to see our grandparents again but more importantly it is so good to see my parents smile again."

Fairy Eimear patted Fidelma gently on the back. "Sit down and have some tea Fidelma."

Fidelma sat down at the table with Fairy Eimear and Fairy Áine when Fairy Caoimhe came in and joined them. "Oh Fidelma, it is so good to see you!" she said as she put her arm around Fidelma before sitting down.

"So Fidelma," smiled Fairy Eimear, "I heard you met Meara!"

"Oh yes!" said Fidelma as she sipped at her tea. "You could have told me she was a mermaid, or a merrow-" she looked at Fairy Áine, "-I could not believe my eyes! I thought I was seeing things!"

Fairy Áine laughed at Fidelma. "Oh I wanted to keep it as a surprise, I would have loved to have seen your face!"

The fairies all giggled, Fidelma looked around at them and began laughing too.

"Meara asked if we could be friends." Fidelma said to the group.

"Oh great," said Fairy Áine, "Meara is so sweet"

"She has such beautiful hair." Exclaimed Fidelma

"Oh, she does, doesn't she?" Fairy Eimear chimed in.

"And she has the most beautiful fluke," said Fairy Caoimhe.

"What is a fluke?" Fidelma asked.

"Oh, that is the name of a merrows tail" explained Fairy Áine "and yes, Meara's is definitely the most beautiful of them all."

"Are there other ones?" asked Fidelma. "I mean, different types of tails? Flukes?"

"Oh yes," replied Fairy Áine, "Each merrow has a different one, they come in lots of different colours, but Mearas is my favourite."

"Are you meeting with her tomorrow Fidelma?" Fairy Caoimhe asked.

"Yes!" answered Fidelma "I'm going to go back to the lakes tomorrow morning."

CHAPTER 5:

It was Wednesday morning and Fidelma was sitting on the same rock she had sat on yesterday with Meara, she had been there about half an hour and still there was no sign of her new friend. It was another beautiful day and the lake looked magnificent as the reflection of the sun made it look like a sea of crystals, but Fidelma was starting to feel bored as she waited, she really wanted to skim some stones but was afraid to, for fear of hitting Meara with a pebble before she even had a chance to surface. Fidelma was contemplating taking a stroll along the shoreline when there was a break in the still water and up rose the beautiful Meara. Fidelma waved happily as she watched Meara glide gracefully through the water towards her.

As Meara pulled herself up onto the rock beside Fidelma she chatted happily as Fidelma was mesmerized once again by her dazzling golden fluke. "I must apologise for my time keeping Fidelma, would you believe my brothers wanted to come with me? I had to go to my parents to get them to speak to them, honestly, sometimes they are unbearable. Do you have brothers Fidelma?"

Fidelma laughed at Mearas bubbly nature. "Yes, I do, I have two brothers, they're younger than me though, I am the eldest. Their names are Brian and Sean, what are your brothers' names?"

"Mon and Crevan," answered Meara rolling her eyes dramatically. "And they're older than me and think they know everything, but they don't."

Fidelma giggled. "Why did they want to come with you?"

Meara looked at Fidelma in wonder "Are you serious? Well, I have told them all about the beautiful Fidelma of course, but you are *my* friend, not theirs." Meara huffed and pouted for a moment. Fidelma smiled fondly as she watched Meara, she found her fascinating.

Suddenly Meara's mood changed. "Oh would you like to come for a swim?" she asked Fidelma excitedly.

Fidelma grimaced. "Oh I am afraid I am not a great swimmer."

"Oh, do not worry about that, I can teach you."

Fidelma wasn't so sure but before she could answer Meara had moved on to another idea. "Or I could come and meet your family? See where your Grandparents live? Oh, I would really love to do that!"

Fidelma looked at Meara in confusion. "Meet my family? How would that work? Wouldn't they notice that you have a tail?"

Meara giggled. "Oh I have legs too Fidelma!" she said matter-of-factly. "Once my fluke dries in the sun it turns into a fine pair of legs and then I have one hour until they turn back into the fluke again!"

Fidelma was speechless, she just stared at the golden fluke as it rested on the rocks.

"I am telling the truth you know." pouted Meara.

"Oh, I believe you." Fidelma said earnestly. "I am just shocked is all, I never imagined." She was thoughtful for a moment. "So you can walk around on land for a full hour? Whenever you want?"

"Whenever I want." sighed Meara. "Also, we have a little red cap back at the kingdom, it allows us to live on land for up to six months at a time if we so wish!"

This statement astonished Fidelma. "Oh my!" she exclaimed "Six months at a time? With legs? That really is amazing!"

Meara shrugged. "I suppose, but nobody ever uses it, we are merrows, we do not have a desire to live on land."

Fidelma shook her head. "I bet your Kingdom is beautiful if you have no desire to leave it!"

Meara smiled fondly at this. "Oh it is Fidelma, oh! I could take you to visit our Kingdom, you would like that wouldn't you Fidelma?"

Fidelma was unsure, she really was not a competent swimmer. "Mmmm maybe." she mumbled non-committedly.

Meara had moved on though. "I should like to go for a walk around the lake, I think that is what we should do on this fine morning Fidelma don't you think?"

And that is exactly what the two girls did, once Meara's fluke had dried out in the sun and her legs appeared, the two friends scurried over the rocks and stones chasing each other in squeals of delight. Fidelma had forgotten what it was like to have some fun, ever since little Nellie disappeared everything seemed so serious and grey. But for the first time in a long time, here in County Kerry, running around over the rocks by the lakes with her new friend who just happened to be a merrow, Fidelma felt her heart soar again.

CHAPTER 6:

Fidelma made her way once again to the spot at the lake where she would meet Meara, she was really enjoying her company. Every morning for the past week Fidelma met with Meara, they would hang out for an hour around the lake and Meara would tell stories of life in her kingdom. In return Fidelma would tell Meara about the village she lived in with her family in County Dublin and the shop where she worked.

Fidelma had just sat down on the rock when she seen the familiar break in the water and Meara appeared. When Fidelma stood up to wave at her friend in greeting she noticed the water breaking again and another head appearing with the same white blonde hair. A male merrow appeared and Fidelma presumed it was one of Meara's brothers. Meara waved happily to Fidelma when she spotted her. "My brother insisted on coming with me today." She said rolling her eyes as they approached the rocks.

Meara pulled herself up onto the rock beside Fidelma and her brother pulled himself onto another nearby rock. "Fidelma this is my big brother Mon." Meara said as an introduction. "Mon this is my good friend Fidelma."

Mon smiled broadly showing a mouthful of perfect pearly white teeth as he extended his hand towards Fidelma. "I am very pleased to finally meet you Fidelma."

Fidelma felt her cheeks flush as she took his hand, "P - Pleased to meet you too." she stammered. Fidelma could not help but to stare at Meara's brother and his beautiful blonde curls and piercing blue eyes, Fidelma had never seen anyone so handsome. Mon too seemed to be mesmerized by Fidelma, they stared at each other for a moment before Meara broke the silence.

"Oh, come on you two, wake up!" Meara waved her hand in front of Mon's face. "Fidelma, I was telling my brothers about your chasing game, we should play it with Mon once our flukes dry out."

Fidelma simply smiled in response, she felt as though she had lost the power of speech. She looked at Mon's tail as he rested it on the rocks beside him, it was different from Meara's, his was a dark blue but turning green at the fin, the scales shimmering in the sunlight too. Fidelma felt very ordinary beside the two merrows, they reminded her of pictures she had seen of Greek Gods in a book she had borrowed from the library one time.

They sat in the sun waiting for the merrows flukes to dry out with Meara chatting away excitedly while Mon and Fidelma stole little glances at each other.

Once the legs were ready Meara jumped up and began running across the rocks, Mon stood up and put his hand out to help Fidelma. "Thank you." she muttered shyly, barely able to make eye contact before taking off after Meara.

Later that evening Fidelma was sitting at the table in An Crann Darach Sean, cup of tea in front of her. Fairies Áine, Eimear and Caoimhe were sitting at the table too, they watched Fidelma as she sat staring into her tea.

"Fidelma?" Fairy Áine called, making Fidelma jump. "You're in a daze, I have called your name three times!"

"Sorry..." said Fidelma shaking her head as if trying to wake herself up. "Sorry I was miles away."

"We noticed." giggled Fairy Caoimhe.

"Want to tell us what you're thinking of?" Fairy Eimear asked.

"Nothing really." fibbed Fidelma. "just daydreaming."

"Did you meet with Meara again today?" Fairy Áine asked. "You two are really becoming good friends, you know we have a portal that can take us to the lakes in a matter of minutes so even when you go back to Dublin you will still be able to visit Meara from time to time."

Fidelma's eyes lit up at this piece of information. "Really? Oh, that would be wonderful."

"Has she taken you to see her kingdom yet?" Fairy Caoimhe asked as she poured more tea.

"Not yet." answered Fidelma. "But I did get to meet one of her brothers today."

"Oh lovely." smiled Fairy Áine "Which one?"

"Mon." answered Fidelma dreamily, and even as she said his name, she could feel the heat rising in her cheeks.

The fairies exchanged knowing looks. "So now we know why you're daydreaming." teased Fairy Eimear.

Fidelma frowned. "What? I don't know what you mean!"

Fairies Eimear and Caoimhe giggled but Fairy Áine was a bit more cautious, she reached over and placed her hand gently over Fidelma's hand as she spoke. "Fidelma he is certainly very handsome, but you realise that nothing can come of it? He is a merrow and as the eldest boy in his family he is destined to be King."

Fidelma pulled her hand away and stood up from the table. "Don't be ridiculous Fairy Áine, I was thinking nothing of the sort!" she said indignantly. "Now if it is alright with you, I am going out to see Ámharach."

Ámharach was Fidelma's beloved and loyal horse and as she approached him, he looked up at her and neighed. *"Fidelma, I am happy to see you!"* Fidelma smiled at her horse, she was always so happy to see him too. When she reached him, she put out her hand and rubbed his face affectionately.

"Do I see a sparkle in your eyes today Fidelma?" Ámharach asked.

"Oh no, not you too." Fidelma said rolling her eyes.

"Oh!" said Ámharach *"Why don't you climb on; we'll go for a walk, and you can tell me all about it."*

And so Fidelma did just that, she told Ámharach all about her trip to Kerry. She spoke about her worries around Fairy Áine visiting her, and all about her encounter with Meara, the treasure chest, and all about Meara's brother Mon. Although Fidelma denied any feelings for Mon to Fairy Áine, she feared that she did indeed have feelings for him and she could not help but hope that he would visit her tomorrow as he promised.

CHAPTER 6:

Fidelma's parents had both headed back to County Dublin after having their well-deserved break in County Kerry, leaving the children behind to spend more quality time with their grandparents. The two boys usually spent their time helping Grandad Ryan and their Uncle Patrick working on the small farm while Fidelma, Nora and Nuala helped Granny Ryan around the house and in the garden. They also did a lot of knitting in the evening and had made a couple of shawls between them. Granny Ryan said when they had made enough, she would take them to the market so they could sell them.

Fidelma was really enjoying being in Kerry, it was a completely different pace of life to the one she had in Dublin, it was so much more peaceful, and the air felt fresher too. Fidelma would come back from her time at the lake and herself and Nora would take Nuala out for a walk, sometimes heading back towards the lakes.

It had now been two weeks since Fidelma had met Mon at the lake, and he had accompanied his sister every day since. The three of them had great fun together and Fidelma felt more comfortable in his company every day. This morning as she walked towards the lakes she could feel a change in the weather, the last couple of weeks had been warm and hazy but this morning felt a little cooler and the clouds were threatening to release a downpour of rain.

Sure enough, not long after Meara and Mon arrived, they were sitting on the rocks when Fidelma noticed the first little drops of rain connect with the lake. "Oh, I am going to have to make a run back I'm afraid." Fidelma said pulling her shawl up over her head.

"Oh no," cried Meara, "but we have only just got here!"

"Why don't we take you to our Kingdom?" Mon suddenly suggested.

Meara quickly jumped on this bandwagon. "Oh yes please, please do Fidelma!"

"What? How am I to get there? I don't have a swimming costume?"

Meara giggled. "You do not need one Fidelma"

"I'm not a good swimmer either." Fidelma protested feeling suddenly nervous.

"Don't worry Fidelma." said Mon. "I promise I will keep you safe."

The rain had started to get heavier, and Meara shrieked as she dived back into the lake excitedly. "Come on Fidelma! Oh, it's so exciting!"

Mon smiled at Fidelma. "Climb on my back and hold on really tight."

Fidelma stood up on the rock where she had been sitting and put her arms around Mon's's neck, nestling into his back.

"Count to three Fidelma." he called back to her. "Then take the deepest breath you can take and hold it."

Fidelma did as she was instructed and before she knew it, they were beneath the lake moving swiftly. She held on tight, holding her breath and shutting her eyes tightly. Just as she felt she could no longer hold her breath, Fidelma felt the pressure of the water drift away from her body as they pierced the surface. Fidelma gasped as she took gulps of air into her lungs.

"Here we are," said Mon gently. Fidelma opened her eyes and looked around her. It looked as if they were on a beach, Mon was walking from the water now and gently dropped her onto the sand.

"Your legs!" was all Fidelma could manage to say as she tried to catch her breath.

Mon chuckled. "Yes, we use our legs here, it is only when we go into your world that we have our tail, or if we are swimming in the water around the kingdom obviously."

Mon stood up tall and pointed towards a castle. The building, which was covered in colourful shells and stones seemed to be in a huge bubble. Outside of the bubble were smaller dwellings, each in their own small bubble. Fidelma looked around her dumbfounded.

"Welcome to our Kingdom." Mon announced.

Fidelma looked at the castle. "Is this where you live?"

"In the castle?" asked Mon. "yes I live here with my family." Mon waved his hand around gesturing the smaller dwellings in their individual bubbles. "...and this is the Kingdom!"

Fidelma was agog as she looked around her with her mouth open. "Do people live in those pretty houses?"

"Of course they do!" came Meara's familiar voice from behind Fidelma. "This is our kingdom Fidelma, it is beautiful is it not?"

Fidelma nodded. "It is like something from a fairy tale, it is the most beautiful thing I have ever seen."

The two merrows smiled at each other before Mon took Fidelma's hand. "Come on." he said, "You should meet our parents."

As the trio walked up to the castle Fidelma looked around her taking it all in, outside of the castles bubble she could see other mermaids swimming about, stopping to chat to each other, it was such a wonderful sight.

Meara skipped on ahead of them excitedly while Mon kept a firm grip of Fidelma's hand and she was more than happy to let him. Suddenly a voice called down to them. "Where have you two been?" A young man appeared at the doorway to the castle, he made his way towards them and Fidelma noticed he was very alike Meara and Mon although she did not think he was as handsome as Mon.

"We have been with Fidelma!" Meara called happily. "And look, we have brought her here for a visit, she is exquisite is she not?"

Fidelma felt her cheeks flush with embarrassment at this compliment.

"So I see." replied the young man as he eyed Fidelma curiously.

"Fidelma this is our brother Crevan." said Mon introducing them.

Fidelma took Crevans offered hand and shook it. "Pleased to meet you Crevan" she said shyly.

"Pleasure" replied Crevan with a smile "Mother and Father are in the Great Hall having tea, you should take Fidelma to meet them."

"Oh, we will, we will" said Meara excitedly as she grabbed Fidelma's hand forcing Mon to let go.

Mon patted Crevan on the back. "Come with us brother."

And the four of them made their way towards the Great Hall of the castle.

As they entered the Great Hall Fidelma gasped at the spectacular surroundings, the walls were adorned with huge paintings of Merrows, Fidelma guessed they were from different generations of the family. The main painting being of the current King and Queen and their three children, all paintings were under water portraits that created captivating images. The great hall was taken up by a long table which at first glance Fidelma imagined could sit about thirty people. At the head of the table sat a regal looking gentleman who was like an older version of both Mon and Crevan except his hair was snow white as was his long curly beard. Sitting beside him was a beautiful woman who had a striking resemblance to Meara, her blonde hair, streaked with snow white strands was piled on top of her head and nestled into it was a dainty gold tiara.

Fidelma immediately curtsied before the King and Queen. "Mother, Father" shrieked Meara excitedly. "This is Fidelma whom we told you about, we have brought her here to visit"

The King nodded his head slightly and the Queen gestured to the empty seats at the table. "Céad mile fáilte Fidelma." the Queen smiled kindly. "You are very welcome to our home, please sit with us."

Fidelma curtsied again to the giggles of an amused Meara. Mon moved forward and gently touched Fidelma's elbow. "No need to keep curtsying Fidelma." he whispered. Fidelma looked up gingerly at the Queen who nodded encouragingly and the four of them made their way to the table and took a seat each. The Queen lifted a tiny bell from the table and gently rang it, a moment later a woman with long white hair braided and wrapped into a pile on top of her head appeared as if from nowhere. "Yes, your highness?" she asked, her eyes darting towards Fidelma and quickly taking her in.

"Can we have some more tea for the children and their guest please?"

"Certainly, your highness." replied the woman as she scurried away again, Fidelma watched as she exited through a door that looked as if it was part of the wall.

"The children tell us you are good friends with Fairy Áine?" The King spoke for the first time.

"Yes." Fidelma answered shyly. "I am the Protector!"

"Well," the Queen smiled "I, Queen Méabh, and my husband King Loch are very pleased to meet you, Meara and indeed Mon have told us all about you."

Fidelma smiled shyly. "It is a pleasure to meet you both and to see your beautiful Kingdom."

"We were very saddened to hear about your sister Nellie." continued the Queen. "If there was anything we could do, but alas, our magic is no match for the evil Balor."

Fidelma felt her eyes fill with tears at the sudden mention of little Nellie and the kindness in Queen Méabh's words. "Thank you," she said, "I do hope I can defeat Balor some day and save little Nellie."

"His day will come!" the King spoke fervently. "But I feel it will be some time before he reappears."

"Yes." Fidelma answered solemnly. "Fairy Áine expressed this worry too, but I will be ready for him."

"Well," smiled the King "I do not doubt that."

CHAPTER 7:

Fidelma had arrived in An Crann Darach Sean and was full of excitement.

"I feel Fidelma has some news for us!" announced Fairy Áine. "Come sit and have some tea."

Fairies Eimear and Caoimhe brought cups and tea to the table as they all sat down and waited eagerly for Fidelma's news.

"Mon and Meara took me to the Kingdom of Leane, it was spectacular!" She exclaimed.

"So, you got to meet the King and Queen?" Fairy Eimear asked.

"I did!" smiled Fidelma. "Oh it was wonderful; they were so kind and welcoming. Mon and Meara showed me all around the castle and I met their brother Crevan too!"

"Well, it sounds like you had a very exciting day." Fairy Áine said, "how did you get to the kingdom, did Meara take you?"

Fidelma reddened a bit as she answered, "Well they both took me, but it was Mon who I went with, I climbed on his back and held on tight, I have to say I was terrified but now I cannot wait to go back again."

"Oh," said Fairy Áine, "Do you think you will go back?"

"Oh yes!" said Fidelma dreamily. "Mon said we could go again tomorrow."

"Be very careful Fidelma." said Fairy Áine. "Meara could get jealous."

Fidelma frowned. "How do you mean?" she asked, "Why would

Meara be jealous?"

"Well," began Fairy Áine "You were *her* friend first remember? she might not want to share you with Mon."

"Don't be silly." Fidelma said shaking her head. "That is madness, I am friends with both, the three of us get along well."

"Just be careful." Fairy Áine repeated her warning.

The next day as Fidelma made her way towards the lake she could see a figure walking along the shore. It was a beautiful sunny morning and Fidelma had left earlier than usual and did not expect the merrows to have arrived yet so she was curious as to who the figure could be. As she got closer, however, she realised it was actually Mon. He must have been there a while because he already had his legs. Fidelma quickened her pace as she wondered why he was so early and why Meara was not with him.

"Hello Fidelma." Mon waved as he turned and saw her approach.

"Hello Mon." Fidelma smiled. "You're early today, where is Meara? Is everything alright?"

Mon looked nervous as he looked down at his bare feet. "I did not tell Meara I was coming here early; I was hoping that you and I could have some time on our own first?"

Fidelma smiled timidly. "I'd like that."

"Shall we go for a walk?" he asked.

Fidelma nodded and the pair continued along the shore, Fidelma stopping to remove her shoes and stockings first.

They walked silently for a moment before Mon spoke again. "Did you enjoy your trip to our Kingdom?"

"Oh yes," Fidelma gushed, "It was wonderful, I still cannot believe I got to see it."

"Our parents really liked you." Mon said suddenly.

Fidelma giggled. "I liked them too, your mother is very kind."

"She is," Mon agreed, "I hope she did not upset you too much talking about little Nellie."

Fidelma shook her head sadly. "It will always upset me to speak about little Nellie, but I don't ever want to stop talking about her."

Mon smiled kindly at Fidelma before gently taking her hand. Fidelma felt safe and secure with him.

"Can I ask where you keep her?" Mon asked gently.

"I keep her with me." Fidelma answered matter-of-factly."I brought her with me to Kerry, before I go to bed, I like to sit outside with her and tell her all about my day, Fairy Áine says she can probably hear me."

"I would really like to meet her."

"Really?" Fidelma said in surprise.

"Of course," Mon said earnestly, "I know how much she means to you."

Fidelma just smiled as she thought that there, in that moment, she never wanted to leave Co. Kerry.

Suddenly Fidelma noticed a break in the still water as Meara emerged from the lake, her face growing thunderous when she spotted Mon with Fidelma.

"Why did you leave without me?" she called crossly to her brother.

Fidelma let go of Mon's hand as he called back to Meara. "I thought you had left already," he fibbed, "I could not find you, so I came on ahead."

"It's true." Fidelma said as Meara approached them. "And I have only just arrived at the lake, so he has been here on his own for a while."

"Hmmm," said Meara eyeing them both suspiciously. "Well do not leave without me again Mon, Fidelma was my friend first."

Fairy Áine's cautious warning came to Fidelma's mind. "Don't fret!" Fidelma reassured Meara. "I am still your friend, but I am Mon's's friend now too."

"Well, I don't think I like it." Meara pouted much to Fidelma's surprise.

"I know." said Fidelma encouragingly. "Why don't we play Hide and Seek?"

Meara cheered up and clapped her hands. "Oh yes please!" she squealed excitedly. "I love Hide and Seek!"

Mon smiled gratefully at Fidelma before announcing that he would be the seeker. He told the two girls to find good hiding spaces.

Meara and Fidelma took off over the rocks in separate directions while Mon covered his eyes and counted to fifty before he called out. "Ready or not, here I come!"

Mon looked around him for a moment, he could see a large rock to his left with a suspicious tuft of white, blonde hair sticking up from the top of it. Smiling to himself, he took off in the opposite direction, climbing over the rocks he soon found Fidelma hiding behind one of the larger ones. Fidelma gasped when she seen him, but Mon put his finger to his lips to shush her before bending down gently and planting a delicate kiss on her forehead. The two stared at each other for a moment before Mon backed away and took off towards the rock where he knew his sister was hiding. Fidelma stood up, feeling like she was in a trance, her hand reached up and touched her forehead and she smiled at the memory of her very first kiss.

Meara

CHAPTER 8:

The next morning Fidelma woke later than usual, everyone else was downstairs and she could hear a lot of excited chatter coming from the kitchen. Fidelma dressed quickly and made her way downstairs, when she got to the bottom step she stopped in awe at the scene before her.

Her grandparents, uncle Patrick and her siblings were all sitting at the table and holding their attention was none other than Meara. She was like an angel sitting among them with her bright blonde hair braided, curving around her shoulder, and wearing a simple but brilliant white dress, she was almost glowing and Fidelma could see her whole family were transfixed by her. Why wouldn't they be, she was beautiful in a way that none of them had ever seen.

Meara jumped up as soon as she seen Fidelma, clapping her hands in the childlike way that she does. "Fidelma you are up! I have come here to meet your family; you have not told them about me."

Fidelma blinked a couple of times as she tried to work out what to say, she let Meara take her hand and lead her over to a seat at the table.

Granny Ryan spoke first. "Fidelma you never mentioned you made yourself a friend here?"

Fidelma looked around at her family who were all staring at her waiting for an answer. "Eh y. .yes" she stammered. "I met Meara down at the lakes."

"We have become such good friends have we not?" Meara added excitedly.

Fidelma nodded. "Yes, such good friends."

"Well," Meara continued. "Fidelma has met my brother Mon whom I am sure she has told you all about, and she has been to my home to meet the rest of our family."

Grandad Ryan frowned. "You never mentioned this Fidelma."

Fidelma looked at her grandparents. "I . . . I," she stammered again.

"You never mentioned Meara or her brother Mon." said Granny Ryan before turning to Meara. "Is your brother older or younger than you Meara?"

"Oh, he is my oldest brother, he is quite taken with Fidelma." Meara grinned.

Fidelma's grandparents turned to look at her now. Fidelma wished the ground would swallow her up. "Oh, I wouldn't say that Meara," she smiled nervously, "we are friends just like you and I."

Grandad Ryan stood up from the table. "All the same, you should not be spending time with this young man without a chaperone"

"Oh Grandad…" Fidelma exclaimed pleadingly. "-It is not like that, Mon and I are friends and that is all, we just go for walks around the lake!"

"Well, he can come here and ask us if he can take you out for a walk the next time." Grandad Ryan said firmly as Fidelma nodded her head contritely.

"Shall we walk down to the lake now Fidelma?" Meara asked innocently and Fidelma honestly could not work out if she even realised what she had just done, was she trying to make trouble for Fidelma or was she merely babbling in the innocent way that she does.

Fidelma left the farmhouse with Meara, and they began walking towards the lakes.

"Why did you come here Meara?" she asked.

"Like I said Fidelma." Meara answered simply. "You have met all my family and I wanted to meet yours too, do not worry, they don't know that I am a merrow."

"But why did you say those things about Mon? You do realise you have caused me some trouble now, don't you?"

Meara stopped walking. "Caused you trouble? Oh, Fidelma how have I?" she asked in such an innocent voice that Fidelma suddenly realised she did not mean any harm. "I was simply telling your family how we are all getting along so well."

Fidelma shook her head. "Yes well, that may be so, but my grandparents would not like me to be spending time with Mon without a chaperone"

"Oh, do not be so silly," laughed Meara, "sure I will be with you both at all times will I not?"

Fidelma shrugged. She bent down to remove her shoes and stockings as they got closer to the lake shore. Meara ran straight into the water. "My hour is almost up Fidelma, I can feel my tail coming back, do you want to come with me to my home?"

Fidelma shook her head. "I don't think so Meara, I might just stay here for a while and then walk back to the farmhouse."

"Alright so Fidelma, see you tomorrow." And with a wave and a splash she disappeared beneath the water.

Fidelma walked towards the larger rocks and sat down on one, resting her feet in the cool still water. She felt a bit worried now, her grandparents would watch her like a hawk and would most likely write to her parents, they would probably send her sister Nora with her to the lakes from now on.

Fidelma's thoughts were interrupted by some movement in the lake, she looked out and saw Mon gliding gracefully through the water, as he got close, he sat on a rock beside her.

"Whatever is the matter Fidelma?" he asked with concern.

Fidelma sighed as she told him about Meara's visit and the things she said to her grandparents.

Mon shook his head angrily. "I don't believe that girl sometimes."

"I don't believe she meant any harm." Fidelma offered.

"You just would not know with Meara." said Mon. "She is very sweet, but she has an awful jealous streak, and she definitely does not like me spending more time with you than she does."

"Well, we should probably say goodbye then." Fidelma said sadly fighting hard to keep the tears at bay.

"What?" Mon said in surprise. "Why would we say goodbye Fidelma?" He then turned and took Fidelma's hands in his ."Fidelma I know we have not known each other long but I do not ever want to say goodbye to you, I love you!"

Fidelma stared into Mon's eyes for a moment before speaking. "I love you too Mon."

They both began laughing awkwardly before Mon spoke again. "I will call to your grandparents house Fidelma and let them see and know me, then we can go for walks together, and if they want us to be chaperoned then that is what we will do because I will not say goodbye Fidelma."

Fidelma felt her heart soar she was so overjoyed by Mon's words, she never wanted to leave his side such were her feelings towards him, but she could not help but wonder what Fairy Áine might say and Mon's parents for that matter.

"What about your parents?" Fidelma asked.

"I will speak to my parents." Mon answered. "They will just want me to be happy Fidelma and that is exactly what I am when I am with you."

Fidelma thought for a moment. "What will you tell my grandparents? They will have a lot of questions for you? What age you are, they will want to know who your family are, what you work at?"

Mon put his arm around Fidelma. "Do not fret Fidelma, I suppose I can't tell them that I am actually two hundred and twenty-one."

Fidelma gasped and pulled away. "What? Two hundred and twenty-one? How is that even possible?"

"Come on Fidelma. Surely you know now how it works, in fact, Fairy Áine and I are the same age, has she never told you this?"

"Indeed, she has not." said Fidelma indignantly.

Mon laughed at Fidelma's reaction. "Do not worry my sweet, sweet Fidelma, I promise you, we will make this work. I shall tell your family I am twenty-one, that I am a fisherman and I live on the other side of the lakes with my family."

Fidelma shook her head. "They will wonder what sort of a name Mon is too, what shall we tell them?"

"Tell them it is short for something else; can you think of a name in your world that it could be short for?" asked Mon

Fidelma thought for a moment before answering. "Eamon? We could say it is short for Eamon!"

Mon smiled. "Eamon, I like it."

"It suits you." Fidelma smiled.

"Eamon and Fidelma." Mon said grinning. "It has a nice ring to it."

CHAPTER 9:

The following morning as Fidelma and Nora were helping Granny Ryan clear up after the breakfast there was a knock on the door and young Brian went to open it. Fidelma's heart skipped a beat when she heard Mon's familiar voice "Hello young man, you must be Fidelma's younger brother, which one are you? Brian or Sean?"

"I'm Brian." answered Brian confidently. "Who are you?"

"My name is Mon, ahem, Eamon," explained Mon, "I am a friend of Fidelma's."

Granny Fidelma ran to the door and shoed Brian outside. "Go get your Grandad." she ordered him. She then looked at the handsome young man standing at her front door. "You are welcome to come inside." she offered as she held open the door "I am Fidelma's grandmother, go sit at the table and I will get you some tea."

Mon walked into the old farmhouse and stopped when he seen Fidelma who had frozen on the spot where she was sweeping, she felt her cheeks flare red as Mon smiled at her. "Good morning Fidelma."

Granny Ryan took the broom from Fidelma. "Well don't just stand there Fidelma, sit yourself down at the table." She then turned to Nora who was standing staring in awe at Mon. "Nora put the water on for some tea."

Mon and Fidelma took their seats at the table sitting facing each other silently as Granny Ryan put some tea out on the table and Nora continued to stand and stare. The front door opened again and in walked Grandad Ryan who walked straight over to the table and addressed Mon. "Are you the young man who has been stepping out with our Fidelma?" he asked.

"I am sir," answered Mon as he stood up from his seat and put his hand out. Grandad Ryan looked Mon up and down for a moment before taking his hand and shaking it.

"Sit down and have some tea." Grandad Ryan said as he took his own seat at the head of the table.

"So, tell me young man," began Fidelma's Grandad as he took a sip of tea. "I believe your name is Mon, what is that now? Is that some sort of a foreign name, is it?"

"No sir," Mon answered confidently. "My name is actually Eamon O'Neill; my sister and brother have always called me Mon for short."

Grandad Ryan thought for a moment. "Are you anything to O'Neills Mills are ye?" he asked.

"No sir," Mon replied politely. "My family are on the other side of the lake, we're a fishing family sir."

"Hmm, fishing is it?" asked Grandad Ryan.

"Yes sir." replied Mon.

Grandad Ryan looked from Mon to Fidelma for a few moments.

"And you want to take our Fidelma out for a walk?"

"I would be honoured if I could take Fidelma out for a walk sir." replied Mon.

"Very well." said Grandad Ryan as Fidelma beamed at Mon. "You can take her for a walk down by the lakes now so you can, but Nora will be down there too with her brother Brian and little sister Nuala so no funny business, do you understand?"

"Yes sir," smiled Mon. "I have the upmost respect for Fidelma."

"Hmmm right so." muttered Grandad Ryan. "Away yous' go so."

And with that Fidelma jumped up and threw her arms around her Grandad. "Thank you so much Grandad."

Grandad Ryan just smiled and patted Fidelma's hand as Granny Ryan ushered Norah, Nuala and Brian out the door.

When they got outside of the farmhouse Mon took Fidelma's hand much to the giggles of Brian and Nuala behind them, but Fidelma did not care one bit, she felt she was floating on air as they walked towards the lakes.

Over the next couple of weeks, a routine was formed. Fidelma would head down to the lake early in the morning after breakfast and meet with Meara for a while, then after lunch, Mon would call for Fidelma and they would go for a short walk together, followed by at least one of Fidelma's siblings.

Granny Ryan urged Fidelma to write to her parents telling them about Mon, so she did and soon received a reply from them to say they would like to meet him and would come back to Kerry for a weekend. Fidelma was anxious about her parents meeting Mon, but she also felt excited.

Some mornings when Meara arrived, she would have Mon with her, and they would take Fidelma back to their Kingdom where Fidelma was becoming a familiar face to everyone.

CHAPTER 10:

It was a Friday morning and Fidelma was down at the lake when Meara and Mon arrived together. "Come with us this morning Fidelma," called Meara from the water as Mon made his way towards the rocks where Fidelma was sitting.

"I cannot stay long this morning," replied Fidelma. "My parents are on the train from Dublin, they will be here at around six o'clock this evening and I promised Granny I would help with dinner."

Mon smiled as he put his hand out to Fidelma. "Come with us Fidelma, we won't keep you long, we promise."

Fidelma smiled and shook her head. "Alright so, just for a little while."

Meara clapped her hands excitedly as Fidelma climbed on Mon's back.

When they arrived at the castle Meara approached Fidelma and put her arms around her. "I will leave you two be for a while Fidelma, I shall see you in the castle soon for some tea."

Fidelma looked at Mon shocked. "What was that all about?" she asked.

Mon shook his head and smiled. "She is just very fond of you Fidelma, as am I." He said as he took Fidelma's hand.

Fidelma smiled up at Mon affectionately. "And I of you."

"And so," began Mon as he opened his hand to reveal a beautiful gold ring with a sparkling blue gem. "I would be honoured if you would be my wife."

Fidelma's hands flew up to her mouth as she gasped. "Oh my!" she exclaimed "Are you serious?"

"I am," smiled Mon, "I love you and I want to marry you, please say yes?"

Fidelma beamed. "Yes! Yes of course I would love to be your wife!" and she threw her arms around him.

Mon gently slipped the ring on Fidelma's finger. "Come," he said, "my parents are waiting, they're eager to hear if you have accepted."

The happy couple quickly made their way inside the castle and into the Great Hall where the King and Queen were waiting with Meara and Crevan. As soon as they walked in Meara jumped up from the table excitedly. "Well?" she asked.

Mon smiled at his family. "She said yes!" he announced, and Meara jumped up and down excitedly squealing and hugging both Mon and Fidelma. Crevan came over and shook Mon's hand before giving Fidelma a hug. The King and Queen had stood up from their seats now too and were offering their congratulations.

Queen Méabh walked over and took Fidelma in her arms. "I am so pleased for you both Fidelma, I can see how happy you make our son."

"Thank you so much," beamed Fidelma. "Mon makes me so happy too, I cannot believe we are going to be married!"

After shaking his sons hand King Loch then put his arm around Fidelma. "Welcome to the family Fidelma."

"Thank you." replied Fidelma.

"I am sure you will make a fine Queen someday."

Fidelma frowned. "Wait," she said, "What?"

"Oh, not to worry," chuckled King Loch. "We have plenty of years left in us yet, but you know, someday, Mon will be King and you my dear, will be his Queen."

Fidelma felt dizzy with confusion as she looked from the King to Mon.

"What is it Fidelma," asked a concerned Mon. "Is something wrong?"

Fidelma shook her head. "I . . I" she stammered as everyone looked to her. "I can't become Queen!" she exclaimed.

"But you must!" squealed Meara.

"Meara be quiet," admonished Mon. "Fidelma whatever do you mean you can't become Queen? You know that I will be King some day!"

Fidelma looked around, all eyes were on her. Queen Méabh put her arm around Fidelma and guided her over to a seat at the table "Come and sit down Fidelma and we can talk about it, please do not upset yourself."

Fidelma took a seat at the table and Mon sat down beside her putting a protective arm around her as Queen Méabh rang her bell for the cook to bring the tea.

Once everyone was settled at the table Queen Méabh spoke again. "Fidelma why don't you tell us what is wrong, and we will see if we can fix it."

Fidelma shook her head sadly, "I am so sorry-" she began, "-I hadn't even thought about what marrying Mon would mean!" she looked to Mon now with tears in her eyes. "I'm so sorry!"

"But I do not understand Fidelma!" exclaimed Mon. "Why?"

"I have seen what losing little Nellie has done to my parents," Fidelma explained. "I could never leave them, it would break their hearts, please you must understand?"

"But what about us Fidelma?" Mon pleaded. "We are meant to be together you and I!"

Queen Méabh put her hand up. "Alright Mon, that is enough, you can see how upset Fidelma is," she said as she turned to Fidelma, "and Fidelma I understand what you are saying. You are a very loyal daughter to be putting your parents' feelings before your own, however I do agree with Mon that you two are meant to be together, so what if we came up with a solution?"

Fidelma wiped the tears from her eyes as she looked to the Queen hopefully. "What sort of solution?" she asked.

"Well," began Queen Méabh, "at the top of my head I am thinking that you could still become Queen, live here in the castle, but you could still visit your parents from time to time. Nobody is asking you to give up your family forever Fidelma."

Fidelma thought for a moment before shaking her head sadly. "I just don't think that would work Queen Méabh, my family would want to visit, to see where we live, I know they would. And my mother dreams of the day she becomes a grandmother, I could not take that away from her." Fidelma looked to Mon now with tears in her eyes. "I am so sorry Mon, really I am, but I think it would be best if I left now."

With that Fidelma stood up from the table, everyone else stood up too, Queen Méabh reached over and took Fidelma's hand. "Please take some time to think about it Fidelma, promise us that?"

Fidelma nodded solemnly. "I promise."

A heartbroken Mon then took Fidelma's hand, and they walked towards the door of the Great Hall, Meara jumped up to follow them, but Crevan put out his hand to stop her. "Leave them Meara, they will want to be alone."

Mon and Fidelma were sitting on the rocks at the lake in silence. Fidelma gently slid the ring from her finger and handed it to Mon.

"You should have this back Mon; I hope you can find it in your heart to forgive me and I hope that someday you will understand."

Mon did not take the ring, instead he took Fidelma's hands in his. "Fidelma I understand now, and it is for this reason that I love you! Your unselfishness, your kindness, your loyalty." He took the ring from Fidelma's hand and slid it back on her finger. "I once told you that I never wanted to say goodbye to you Fidelma, and I meant it, and so I have decided that we *will* marry, and I will come with you to Dublin, and we will set up a life there together."

Fidelma pulled away from Mon in shock. "What are you talking about Mon? You cannot live in our world?"

Mon shook his head. "That is not entirely true Fidelma. We have something at the castle, it is called a cohuleen druith, it is a magic red cap, and it allows us to spend up to six months at a time in your world, I would have to wait another six months before I could use it again to come back to you but, Fidelma, I could come back to you, again and again!"

Fidelma stared at Mon aghast. "Mon, I cannot ask you to do that? You are to be King! What sort of King would you be if you were only in your kingdom for six months at a time?" she asked.

Mon took Fidelma's hands in his again. "But that's it Fidelma, I wouldn't *be* King! I will abdicate, give up the throne." Fidelma began shaking her head at this revelation, but Mon continued. "I would Fidelma, being King would mean nothing to me anyway if I cannot have you as my Queen!"

"I cannot allow you to do such a thing." Fidelma cried desperately.

"Don't you understand Fidelma?" pleaded Mon, "I have to, I will not say goodbye to you, and if you will still have me, I want to be your husband here in your world."

Fidelma was overwhelmed. "What about your parents Mon? what will they say? They won't allow it; they will hate me!"

Mon smiled. "They could not hate you Fidelma, and they have

another son, I am sure Crevan would be only too happy to step into my shoes and become King."

"How would it work?" Fidelma asked, "When you must go back for six months, what would we tell people? What would we tell my family?"

Mon thought for a moment "Well," he began "they think I am a fisherman, don't they?" Fidelma nodded. "So, then we tell them that I have to go back to sea every six months, it won't be much of a lie."

Fidelma was still sceptical though, she was not sure it would work but Mon was sure, and he pleaded with her.

"You could come visit me when I am back in the kingdom Fidelma, you know there is a portal near An Crann Darach Sean?"

Fidelma nodded slowly, so many things racing through her mind.

"Fidelma, we could make this work, I just know we can. Let me come and meet your parents this evening, I will ask your father for your hand in marriage."

Fidelma thought for a few minutes as she considered Mon's idea, she then took the ring off and handed it back to Mon. "You better hold onto the ring so until you get permission from my father to marry me"

Mon's face burst into a smile. "Do you mean it?" he asked.

"I do," smiled Fidelma and Mon grabbed her in an emotional embrace.

Fidelma pulled away from Mon after a couple of minutes with a serious look on her face. "You need to make sure your parents are happy to allow you to do this though Mon, promise me you will get their blessing first?"

Mon leaned in and kissed Fidelma gently on her forehead. "I promise you Fidelma."

CHAPTER 11:

Fidelma was helping Granny Ryan set the table for her parents' arrival, they were slicing up some bread and cheese when the door opened, and Fidelma's Uncle Patrick arrived back with her parents coming in behind him. Fidelma and her siblings ran to her parents and there was great excitement as they hugged.

Granny Ryan brought the tea to the table. "That's enough now, your parents must be exhausted after their journey let them take the weight off now." She ushered Fidelma's parents to the table.

"Nora take the children out to play in the field for a bit." Granny Ryan said as Fidelma, her parents, uncle Patrick and Grandad Ryan took seats at the table.

Peter Ryan wasted no time getting straight to the point. "Fidelma who is this young man you've been stepping out with?"

Fidelma gulped some of her tea before answering. "His name is Eamon O'Neill Daddy and I love him." She stated simply to a surprised audience.

Grandad Ryan shook his head. "Well that escalated!"

"Now Fidelma," Mary Ryan spoke with an air of caution. "I know you might think that you love this young man, but you hardly know him, you need to be very careful about making such declarations."

"But Mammy I do love him," protested Fidelma, "and he loves me too!"

Before anyone could say anymore there was a knock on the door. Granny Ryan got up to answer it, there was silence at the table as everyone heard the voice at the door. "Good evening Mrs Ryan, I was wondering if I could speak with Mr Ryan please, Fidelma's father." Mrs Ryan turned to pass on the request, but Peter Ryan had already stood up. "Send the young man in Mammy," he said.

Fidelma blushed as she watched Mon walk into the farmhouse and nod respectfully at her family. She was thinking how much he stood out in what suddenly seemed like drab surroundings.

"Take a seat Eamon." Peter Ryan gestured to an empty chair at the table.

"Thank you, sir," said Mon as he sat down, smiling at Fidelma.

"What can I do for you?" Peter Ryan asked their guest.

"Well, I was hoping that you and I could talk?" replied Mon.

"We can," said Peter Ryan, "go ahead Eamon, you can speak freely here."

Mon looked around the table suddenly looking nervous.

"Well sir," he began, clearing his throat. "I am in love with your daughter Fidelma and I was hoping to gain your permission to ask Fidelma to be my wife?"

There was an audible gasp around the table, Fidelma was practically beaming at Mon she felt so happy.

Peter Ryan looked around the table as everyone watched him expectantly, it was indeed unusual for a father to be asked for his daughters' hand in marriage in front of so many family members let alone the actual daughter.

"Tell me Eamon," he began, "will you be able to provide for my daughter?"

"I will sir," Mon nodded. "I am a fisherman."

Peter Ryan nodded slowly as he mulled it over before standing up from the table. "Well I suppose you two will want to be going for a wee walk so?"

Mon stood up now too. "We would very much like to sir," smiled a happy Mon.

Peter Ryan walked around and shook Mon's hand. "You have my blessing son."

Mon turned to Fidelma and took her hand. "Shall we?"

Fidelma blushed as she looked at her mother who looked like she was about to cry, she stood up and hugged her father. "Thank you Daddy!" before taking Mon's hand and heading for the door.

CHAPTER 12:

The happy couple headed down towards the lake, hand in hand. Fidelma was feeling like she was walking on air she was so elated. When they got to the shore, Mon took the ring from his pocket and gently slid it onto Fidelma's finger, the couple gazed into each other's eyes for a moment before putting their arms around each other.

"How did your parents react?" Fidelma asked, breaking away from their embrace.

"Fidelma my parents are happy for us." Mon replied. "They did take a little bit of convincing; they had hoped you would come and live in our kingdom and be queen and deep down I think they are hoping maybe someday you still will, but for now they are happy to let me give up the crown, pass it to Crevan."

"I see." said Fidelma thoughtfully. "-and what about Crevan, is he happy to be King?"

"Are you serious?" laughed Mon "He gets to be King of Leane!"

Mon sat down on a rock. "Come on Fidelma, let us go to the kingdom now, our parents would like to celebrate our engagement."

It was later that evening and Fidelma had just arrived at An Crann

Darach Sean with an extremely curious Fairy Áine. Fidelma had told her that she had some exciting news but wanted to wait and tell everyone together.

Fairy Áine clapped her hands and called out. "Gather around fairies, Fidelma has some news for us!"

Fidelma and Fairy Áine sat down at the table as Fairy Eimear brought over some tea and cups, it didn't take long for the table to be surrounded by many more fairies, all eager to hear of Fidelma's news.

Fairy Áine looked at Fidelma who was positively glowing. "Well go ahead Fidelma, don't keep us in suspense for a moment longer."

Fidelma's smile spread across her face as she produced her left hand with the beautiful engagement ring on her finger for all to see. "Mon and I are engaged to be married," she announced to gasps from all around the table.

There were claps and squeals of delight as the fairies rushed at Fidelma to offer their congratulations and get a closer look at her ring.

Fidelma was caught up in the excitement but as she turned to Fairy Áine she noticed she was not joining in with the celebrations.

"Fairy Áine what is it?" Fidelma asked her friend. "Aren't you happy for us?"

Fairy Áine placed her hand on Fidelma's. "Dear Fidelma, I am happy if you are happy, but I must ask, are you sure? Are you both sure? This is a huge decision, where will you live?"

"Mon is going to come to live with me in Dublin." replied Fidelma simply.

"He is giving up his crown?" asked Fairy Áine in shock.

"He loves me!" said Fidelma.

"And I do not doubt that Fidelma," answered Fairy Áine gently, "but Fidelma have you thought about what this could mean? What effects this could have on both our world and your world?"

"We aren't hurting anyone Fairy Áine." replied Fidelma firmly. "-but our love is so strong, we need to be together, Mon's parents have given us their blessing."

"Yes well, sometimes Fidelma, love is simply not enough, believe me, I know."

Fairy Áine got up from the table and walked away from a confused Fidelma. Fairy Caoimhe came over and put her hand on Fidelma's shoulder. "Do not worry Fidelma," she soothed, "Fairy Áine is just worried, but she is happy for you both at the same time."

"I don't get it." said Fidelma. "What did she mean by what she said that she should know? What is she talking about?"

"Well," said Fairy Caoimhe "I will tell you another time but let me just say that Fairy Áine was once in love but chose the crown and her family instead, although if you asked me, I would say she has regretted her decision."

"How so?" asked Fidelma.

"Well sometimes Fidelma," said Fairy Caoimhe, "It is possible to have both." and she smiled affectionately at Fidelma.

CHAPTER 13:

The summer was coming to an end, and it was nearly time for Fidelma and her siblings to return home to Dublin. There were mixed feelings about their return, they were all looking forward to getting back to their parents, their home, and their friends but at the same time each of them had loved their time in Co. Kerry, spending time with their grandparents, being so close to the lakes and the freedom of the countryside.

Fidelma, in particular, was feeling a mix of emotions at returning home, she was certainly sad to be leaving Co. Kerry. As much as she had always loved trips to Kerry to see her Grandparents, the county now held a special place in her heart as the place where she first met the merrows and her beloved Mon. But Fidelma was also excited at the new life that awaited her in Dublin, she had a wedding to organise, and she needed to find a place for them to live. She thought about what Fairy Áine had said to her, but Fidelma was confident with their decision, she knew it would not be easy, but they would be together and that was all that mattered.

There was great excitement back in Dublin over the next few weeks as Fidelma and Nora were busy organising the wedding. Fidelma's Uncle Michael said herself and Mon could move into the room above the shop, he told them they could have it for one year as a wedding present to give them time to save for a house. Fidelma just could not believe how happy she felt, every day after work she would go to the room upstairs that would be their first home and clean it in preparation.

It was just six weeks until Fidelma and Mon would be wed in the local chapel near Fidelma's home in Co. Dublin and then they planned on having a traditional ceremony back in Old Ireland which was being organised by the fairies.

Fidelma had told her family that she was going to go against tradition and carry on working in the shop for a while after she was married until they were set up. She was beginning to worry about how they would manage for money with Mon away every six months; Fidelma knew she should discuss this with Mon but she was afraid to burst the bubble of happiness they were in, she knew that Mon had promised her father that he would be capable of providing for Fidelma but she was unsure exactly how he planned on doing this and so she vowed to bring it up with him later this evening when she met him.

CHAPTER 14:

Fidelma arrived to an unusually quiet An Crann Darach Sean. "Where is everyone?" she asked Fairy Áine who had gone straight to the fire to make some tea.

"Oh they're all very busy working on an extremely important project." Fairy Áine answered nonchalantly.

"Fairy Áine what are you up to?" giggled Fidelma.

Fairy Áine smiled at her friend. "We'll have some tea first and then I'll take you out to see."

Fidelma began helping her friend get the tea ready, they were just about to sit down at the table when the door opened and fairies Eimear and Caoimhe came in.

"Oh Fidelma you're here already!" exclaimed Fairy Eimear.

"Yes," replied Fairy Áine, "we were just having some tea before I take Fidelma outside to see what you are all up to!"

"Yes, I am most curious now." Fidelma smiled.

"Well, you will just have to wait and see," smiled Fairy Caoimhe affectionately as she filled two cups with tea.

The four friends sat companionably around the table drinking their tea and chatting. Fidelma was filling them in on the work she had done in the room above the shop to make it feel like a home for herself and Mon.

When they had finished their tea Fairy Áine stood up. "Alright Fidelma, let's take a walk outside."

The friends made their way outside and out across the field, in the near distance Fidelma could just about make out what the fairies special project was. As they got closer Fidelma felt herself well up with emotion, the fairies had built her a wooden alter for her wedding ceremony.

"Oh, Fairy Áine it really is magnificent." Fidelma gushed as she stood up into the wooden carving.

Fairy Áine smiled at her friend with a glint in her eye. "The fairies have worked tirelessly on this for you Fidelma, you mean the world to us, and we wanted to do something special for you and Mon, we will decorate it with ivy and flowers on the day."

Fidelma turned to Fairy Áine. "Thank you so much," she looked around at the rest of the fairies, "Thank you all so, so much you have no idea what this means to me."

"You are more than welcome Fidelma," said Fairy Caoimhe.

"We will decorate it with ivy to protect you from evil," said Fairy Eimear.

"And bluebells for everlasting love!" smiled Fairy Caoimhe.

"Not that you need any help with that," said Fairy Áine, "anyone can see how in love you and Mon are!"

"You girls are truly the best friends anyone could ever ask for," said Fidelma.

After a short while Fidelma took Ámharach to the portal that would take her to Killarney, she chatted away to her horse as they rode through the fields eventually arriving at the small cave.

"I will wait for you here Fidelma," said Ámharach as Fidelma dismounted.

Fidelma patted her beloved horse on his neck before turning around to see Mon come out through the cave, pulling the hawthorn bush out of his way, he smiled broadly when he seen Fidelma.

The pair embraced before heading into the cave to go visit Mon's family. When they got into the cave Mon stopped to pick up a sharp rock.

"What's that for?" asked Fidelma

"Making our mark!" exclaimed Mon as he began carving a love heart into the wall of the cave, on one side he put his initials and on the other side, Fidelma's.

"Now," he announced when he was done, "Our love will be marked here forever!" and he put his arm around Fidelma as they made their way to the other side of the cave.

Fidelma and Mon were sitting having tea and cake with Meara, Crevan and the King and Queen.

"So Fidelma," announced Queen Méabh, "King Loch is going to use his magic to allow us to attend your wedding in your world, we will be able to stay for six hours before needing to return to the kingdom."

"Oh, that is marvellous news!" exclaimed Fidelma as she turned to Mon. "Mon isn't that fantastic?"

"It is," Mon nodded, "it will be a perfect day."

"We are all so excited Fidelma." Meara chimed in.

"Oh, so am I" said Fidelma. "I cannot believe we are actually getting married!" and she smiled lovingly at Mon.

Mon reached over and took Fidelma's hand, he squeezed gently it before kissing it. "I am the luckiest man in the world" he smiled "both worlds."

King Loch cleared his throat, attracting everybody's attention. "I would like to say a few words here now whilst it is just us."

There was silence around the table, King Loch continued. "First of all I would like to reassure you both that you have our blessing, that you Mon, have our blessing in your decision to abdicate the throne should you stick with your decision. Your mother and I always believed that you would make a fine king someday, but we also believe now in you and Fidelma and we are sure that Crevan will also make a fine King when the time comes, plus you will be on hand every six months to perhaps offer him some guidance."

Mon smiled gratefully at his father.

"Secondly," continued King Loch, "Fidelma I am sure you must have wondered how Mon will provide for you and your prospective family."

Fidelma went to protest this, but King Loch put his hand up to stop her. "Please Fidelma let me finish, we are the King and Queen of this kingdom as you know, and of course, it comes with plenty of advantages, one of which is our wealth. That treasure chest that Meara gave you was one of many we have here at the castle, however, the rest of them are filled, filled with gold and jewels. We would like to gift one of those treasure chests to yourself and Mon, in your world it would be enough to keep good food on your tables and a good roof over your heads for as long as you both shall live!"

Fidelma gasped and Mon stood up from his seat and walked over to his parents. "I cannot thank you both enough," he said as they embraced him, "for everything."

CHAPTER 15:

2017

Fidelma

Young Fidelma stood up from the table in An Crann Darach Sean where she had been sitting with Fairies Áine, Eimear and Caoimhe as they told her the story of her beloved Granny and her estranged Grandfather. The fairies watched now as Fidelma began pacing around the room.

"Unbelievable," she muttered to herself over and over again before stopping and facing the fairies. "So, my Granny fell in love with a merrow?"

"They were both so in love with each other Fidelma." exclaimed Fairy Caoimhe.

"And she married him? She married a merrow? A prince?" Fidelma half asked half exclaimed.

Fairy Áine stood up and approached Fidelma, taking her hands in her own. "Fidelma you have to understand, your granny had been through the most unimaginable trauma with little Nellie, she was strong, a true warrior, but all of a sudden she needed to be taken care of, and Mon just happened to be the one to do that."

Fidelma shook her head. "I don't understand why she didn't tell me, why she didn't tell anyone!"

Fairy Áine looked back at the other fairies before she answered. "Fidelma, she couldn't tell anyone, surely you understand that. Your granny had to protect our world, just as you do."

Fidelma was quiet and thoughtful for a moment before she spoke again. "So, what happened then? If they were both so in love, if Mon had the blessing of his family, if he had this magic cap to allow him to live in our world, what happened? How come he left my Granny? How come he left his children? My Mam?"

Fairy Áine guided Fidelma back towards the table while Fairy Eimear refilled the cups with fresh tea.

"Mon never stopped loving your granny," explained Fairy Áine. "Their arrangement was working well, they were living in Dublin, they had a lovely new home beside your grannys parents' house, and they shared the back garden. Mon loved growing the vegetables and helping with the hens, it was all new to him, so different to his life back in his kingdom, however, back to his kingdom he did go, every six months."

Fidelma shook her head again trying to make sense of it. "How did they explain that? How could he just go off for six months at a time?"

"Times were different then Fidelma, that Mon would head off as a fisherman for six months at a time was quite plausible."

"Ok," conceded Fidelma. "So why did he leave then?"

Fairy Áine shook her head sadly. "Meara."

Fidelma frowned. "Meara?"

"She became enraged with jealousy and destroyed the cap that allowed Mon to live in your world, he could never return once it was gone." Said Fairy Áine solemnly.

"That makes no sense," said Fidelma. "I thought Meara was happy for them"

"She was," shrugged Fairy Eimear. "That's what made it even more shocking for everyone."

"Hold on," said Fidelma thoughtfully. "My Mam is the youngest in her family, there's six girls in the family, the eldest is my Auntie Mary and she's 72!"

The fairies all stared at Fidelma, waiting for her to make her point.

Fidelma rolled her eyes. "My Mam is only 48, that's a 24-year difference."

"Quite common in those days Fidelma," explained Fairy Áine.

"No, I know that," exclaimed Fidelma. "But do you not think it strange that it took Meara nearly thirty years after my granny and Mon got married to act on her jealousy?"

The fairies were silent for a moment before Fairy Áine spoke. "I have no explanation for that Fidelma, I just know that it was Meara who destroyed the cap."

"Did she admit to it?" asked Fidelma

"No," answered Fairy Caoimhe

"She always proclaimed her innocence," offered Fairy Eimear.

The fairies all looked at each other.

"King Mon was always convinced it was Meara, he banished her from the castle, she now lives in the Upper lake."

"And what did you all think?" Fidelma asked the fairies.

"We believed King Mon knew best, she is his sister after all." Said Fairy Áine.

"What about my granny?" asked Fidelma "What did she think?"

"Your granny never thought Meara had anything to do it, she loved Meara, they were very close, and she found it hard to believe Meara would betray her in such a way."

"So what? You just left it at that? Even though granny didn't think it was Meara?"

"Well, it wasn't up to us Fidelma," said Fairy Áine gently. "Your grandfather and indeed his brother Crevan were sure it was Meara."

"And had Crevan become King before that?" Fidelma asked.

"Yes, Crevan had been King for a few years when the cap was destroyed." explained Fairy Caoimhe.

"And so, once the cap was destroyed, was Crevan happy to let Mon take over as King?"

"Oh, he was more than happy," said Fairy Caoimhe. "He knew Mon would make a great King."

Fidelma looked around at the fairies. "Does nobody think that this is strange?"

"Fidelma, it was a long time ago," explained Fairy Áine. "There were other things happening, we all just got on with it."

"Just got on with it?" asked Fidelma exasperated. "What about my granny? Was she expected to just get on with it? She lost the love of her life!"

Fairy Áine put her arm around Fidelma "She did not lose him though Fidelma, she lost the ability to live with him, she visited him regularly."

Fidelma glared at Fairy Áine. "My Mam lost him; she never even knew her father."

"I'm sorry Fidelma," said Fairy Áine. "But I'm not sure what you want me to say."

"When was the last time anyone spoke to Meara?" asked Fidelma

"Nobody has seen her since she was banished to the Upper Lake," said Fairy Eimear.

"Not even Mon?" asked Fidelma.

"Especially not Mon." said Fairy Caoimhe.

Fidelma sighed. "This has been a lot to take in, I think I'll head home now if that's ok?"

"Of course," said Fairy Áine standing up from the table.

CHAPTER 16:

Fidelma was in town shopping with Aaron. He had followed Fidelma as she traipsed around the shops without buying anything.

"Will we go for some lunch?" Aaron asked Fidelma

"I'm not that hungry," answered Fidelma. "But tea and cake would be nice, what do you reckon?"

"Ah you don't have to ask me twice." replied Aaron, winking.

They walked to the nearest coffee shop and went in. After spending a few minutes examining the cakes on display they placed their order and sat down at a table looking out on Henry Street.

They sat in silence for a moment before Aaron spoke. "Do you want to tell me what's wrong Fidelma?" he asked.

"What do you mean?" Fidelma frowned.

Aaron shrugged. "You've hardly spoken since we got on the bus a couple of hours ago Fidelma, I know you and I know when something is bothering you."

"Ah it's nothing Aaron," said Fidelma

"Well obviously it's not nothing if I can see that it's bothering you," replied Aaron.

Fidelma thought for a moment before answering. "I found out something over the weekend about my Granny, well, about my Grandad actually"

"Right," said Aaron "the Grandad that you knew nothing about when you were doing your family tree?"

"That's the one," smiled Fidelma

"Is it something bad?" asked Aaron as the waitress came over and placed their tea and cakes on their table in front of them.

Fidelma shook her head, then smiled and thanked the waitress.

"It's not bad, it's just that nobody knows, it's a secret and I don't know what to do with it."

Aaron had his mouth full of cake as he stirred the milk into his tea, so he took a moment to answer.

"Did your granny know about this secret?"

Fidelma sighed. "Yes, I suppose you could say it was her secret."

"Well then I guess you have to respect that your Granny wanted to keep it a secret."

Fidelma smiled fondly at Aaron. "Oh Aaron the wise one," she joked.

Aaron shrugged. "If the cap fits."

Fidelma was waiting patiently for Fairy Áine to arrive, she could not stop thinking over things since the weekend, she felt like her head would explode. She had enjoyed her day with Aaron in town, Aaron was more than her boyfriend, he was her best friend, the one she always went to when she had a problem and he was always a great listener, so she hated that she couldn't properly confide in him today.

Fairy Áine arrived and flew up to kiss Fidelma on her cheek.

"How are you, my friend?" she asked

"Well, I'm still full of questions," said Fidelma

"I know," smiled Fairy Áine. "I suppose that's to be expected, so I thought we would go and see King Mon today."

Fidelma's face lit up at this. "Oh yes, that would be great Fairy Áine thank you."

CHAPTER 17:

Fidelma and Fairy Áine were making their way to the portal for Killarney on board Dílís. When they arrived at the cave Fidelma climbed down from her horse and took some oats out of her satchel for him. "We won't be too long boy," she said as she patted him on the neck.

"No hurry Fidelma," replied Dílís.

Fidelma pulled the hawthorn bush back and walked through into the cave, it was a bit brighter in there since the last time she was in. As they walked through, Fidelma thought about the last time she'd been in the cave and remembered the love heart scratched into the rock with the initials she couldn't make out, she looked for it again and this time the initials were clear, **M O'N** and **F R**. Fidelma ran her hand over the carving and felt her eyes well up with emotion, her grandparents initials, they were so in love, their story was such a true love story with tragedy thrown in. She suddenly thought of how lucky her granny was to have someone who knew about her other life, Fidelma wished she could share her other life with Aaron, but she knew she would never be able to, he wouldn't understand, wouldn't believe her.

Fidelma's thoughts were interrupted by her little fairy friend fluttering beside her. "Are you ready to keep going?"

"Yes," replied Fidelma. "Sorry I was lost in thought."

The two friends continued through the cave until they came through the other side, out into the bubble which contained King Mon's castle. They began to make their way up to the entrance when the door opened and King Mon stepped outside, Fidelma stopped in her tracks, herself and King Mon locked eyes for a moment, then King Mon began to make his way down towards them, he stopped in front of them. "Fidelma," he started. "I am so sorry." Fidelma looked at the man standing in front of her, then she went over and put her arms around him. "Hello Grandad."

Fairy Áine and Fidelma were sitting at the table in the Great Hall with King Mon and little Nellie, the King had called for cook to come and serve them some tea and cake.

"So, what will I call you?" asked Fidelma. "King Mon?"

"I liked when you said Grandad," smiled King Mon, "I have lost out on so much, your mother was just a baby when the cap was destroyed, I still got to see my beloved Fidelma but I missed my children so much, missed them calling me Daddy," King Mon shook his head sadly. "So I would be honoured for you to call me Grandad."

Fidelma smiled at King Mon. "Ok Grandad."

Fidelma took a drink of her tea and cleared her throat before speaking again. "Grandad do you mind me asking you about the cap?"

"Not at all," said King Mon. "Although there isn't much to tell, it provided me with the magic to live in your world for half the year and when Meara destroyed it, I was trapped here forever."

"But how did you know it was Meara?" Fidelma asked.

King Mon sighed. "Well I didn't at first but then Crevan had mentioned that he had seen her with the cap."

"But why do you think Meara would do such a thing after such a long time? It doesn't make sense?"

King Mon shrugged. "Meara never married, I think she was jealous of us having the children, maybe your mother being born was the icing on the cake!"

"Have you spoken to her?" asked Fidelma

King Mon shook his head. "No, not in many years, I banished her to the Upper lake so now she refuses to speak to me or to Crevan."

"How do you know?" asked Fidelma

"Crevan has reached out to her a few times over the years, but she has rebuked his efforts, it is so upsetting, our parents would be sad to see Meara estranged from us."

Fidelma shook her head. "Well it is very sad alright, but it really doesn't make any sense, don't you think?"

King Mon smiled at Fidelma. "You are just like your grandmother Fidelma, she too wanted to believe that Meara wasn't to blame, it is hard when someone you love betrays you."

Fidelma was silent for a moment as she sipped at her tea as King Mon watched her.

"Your grandmother would be extremely proud of you Fidelma," said King Mon. "I heard about how you took the evil Balor down, you were magnificent."

Fidelma felt her cheeks flush at the praise. "Thank you," she said quietly as she thought back to the battle with Balor, the visit to An Chailleach Bhéara and her encounter with Ellén Trechend, when a thought suddenly occurred to her.

"Eh Grandad?" she started. "Something happened to me when I came up against Ellén Trechend."

King Mon leaned forward in his seat, "Yes Fidelma, I heard about that," he looked at Fidelma for a moment before continuing. "I would say your grandmother's gift is not the only one you have inherited."

Fidelma blinked. "wait, you mean?"

"Yes Fidelma, I think it is possible that you are part merrow."

Fidelma shook her head in disbelief.

"There really is no other explanation," King Mon continued.

Fidelma looked at Fairy Áine. "I did suspect as much," explained the fairy, "but the time was not right to tell you about your grandfather, about your bloodline."

King Mon cut in. "Fidelma do you understand what this means?"

"Please don't tell me I'm going to grow a tail," pleaded Fidelma half laughing.

King Mon laughed lightly. "No Fidelma, you can breathe underwater though but that is not what I meant. You have Royal blood Fidelma, a lineage that goes back thousands of years."

Fidelma was stunned, she did not know what to say.

"Merrows don't have magic as strong as the fairies," continued King Mon. "But we do possess some magic, we will have to see if you have inherited any of that."

Fidelma shook her head. "Oh believe me I do not have any magic."

"Maybe none that you know of!" said King Mon.

Fidelma was silent.

Fairy Áine leaned across and touched Fidelma's arm. "You have had a lot to take in Fidelma, I think you should go home now."

CHAPTER 18:

Fidelma was sitting at the desk in her bedroom, finishing off her homework when she heard the doorbell go, she looked at her watch, it was probably Aaron, he said he would call around six o'clock so they could go for a walk. Fidelma shouted down the stairs. "I'll be down in a minute!" and she packed away her homework and pulled on her hoodie before heading downstairs.

"It's just started to rain Fidelma," said Aaron as she was coming down the stairs.

"Ah no." Fidelma moaned.

"Go into the kitchen and have some tea," offered Mrs Doyle. "I made a Victoria sponge earlier yous' can have a slice of that."

"Ah nice one," smiled Aaron rubbing his hands together, "you make the best Victoria sponge Mrs. Doyle"

The pair made their way into the kitchen and Fidelma filled the kettle with water and switched it on.

"So, are you feeling a bit better about things today Fidelma?" Aaron asked as he cut two slices from the cake.

"Ah yeah," smiled Fidelma. "I'm actually feeling much better about it all now."

"Do you wanna talk about it?" asked Aaron "Or is it too secretive?"

Fidelma sighed, she wished she could talk about it. "Too big a secret I'm afraid Aaron, sorry."

"Hey, that's ok, don't be sorry." Aaron said as he handed Fidelma a slice of cake.

Fidelma took her cake and smiled at Aaron, she popped a couple of teabags into the teapot and waited for the kettle to boil.

"So, are you going to have a party for your birthday?" Fidelma asked.

"Nah," answered Aaron, "I think 16th birthday parties are something girls do, might wait and have something for my 18th instead."

Fidelma shrugged. "We should go out for it though, cinema and food?"

"Yeah," said Aaron, "my Mam will just do my favourite dinner for me on the day, but you know me, I'll be ready to eat again a couple of hours later."

Fidelma smiled. "Lasagne?"

Aaron smiled back. "Lasagne, coleslaw, and home-made chips, sure what could be better?"

Later that evening Fidelma arrived at An Crann Darach Sean.

"How are you Fidelma?" asked Fairy Caoimhe as Fidelma walked in.

"Yeah, I'm still trying to get my head around everything but I'm fine," answered Fidelma.

"Will you have some tea?" asked Fairy Eimear.

"Actually, I was hoping I could go out to Dílís," said Fidelma, turning to Fairy Áine. "I just feel like I could do with the headspace for a bit."

"Of course, Fidelma, take all the time you need." Fairy Áine gave Fidelma a brief hug before taking her outside and making her human size again.

Fidelma gave Fairy Áine a quick wave and made her way towards Dílís. As she got closer to him, he sensed her arrival. *"Fidelma! Great to see you, are you well?"*

"All the better for seeing you Dílís," smiled Fidelma. "Fancy going for ride?"

"Hop on!"

No sooner had Fidelma climbed up onto Dílís when they took off at full speed. They galloped through the field, Fidelma's hair whipping across her face as the wind rushed past them. This was just what Fidelma needed, she was so lucky to have Dílís, dashing through the fields like this was so therapeutic. They had been riding for a while when Dílís decided to slow down to a trot. In the distance Fidelma could see a forest.

"Is that Leprechaun Forest up ahead?" Fidelma asked.

"It is Fidelma," answered Dílís. *"You're getting to know your way around here now."*

Suddenly Fidelma noticed a man emerge from the trees, he looked vaguely familiar.

"Dílís, do you know who that man is? He looks familiar to me"

"That's Padraig," explained Dílís, *"He's a friend of the leprechauns, a protector like you Fidelma, but I don't think you two have met."*

Fidelma frowned, the man was a good distance away but something about him was familiar. "Can we go over and meet him Dílís?"

"Of course we can!" and Dílís took off in the direction of the man, who was bending down now and seemed to be picking flowers.

As they approached the old man Fidelma called out to him. "Excuse me!"

The old man stood up and turned around, Fidelma nearly fell off her horse in shock. "Whoa boy!" she brought Dílís to a stop.

"Pat?" Fidelma asked as she climbed down from her horse.

"Lovely to see you again young Fidelma," said the old man.

Fidelma smiled. "I can't believe it's you, I didn't realise you were a protector too?"

"You never asked," answered Pat simply.

Fidelma shrugged. "Fair enough, but Fairy Áine had said she did not know who you were, yet Dílís knew you."

"Ah," Pat said, "You would have mentioned me as Pat I presume, all here know me as Padraig."

Fidelma shook her head. "Wow, all this time you were here too, that's amazing."

Old Pat tipped his old tweed cap to Fidelma then turned around and continued to pick the flowers.

"Who are the flowers for?" Fidelma asked curiously.

"One of the wee men has a toothache, rubbing the leaf of the primrose flower on it for a few minutes will relieve the pain"

Fidelma raised her eyebrows. "Oh I didn't know that."

There was silence from Pat as he continued to pick the flowers, he was obviously a man of few words.

"Listen I wanted to thank you for your help with the children of king Lír." Fidelma said to his back.

Old Pat stood up and turned around to Fidelma. "You're welcome young Fidelma, I felt it was important to help you."

"Did you know my granny well?"

"I knew her," answered Pat. "Not very well though"

"Oh right, well if it were not for you, I might not have broken Aoife's spell and she was becoming extremely dangerous, and not just for me"

"Oh, I know," said old Pat. "It wasn't just you and *your* family who were in danger, I had to help."

Fidelma nodded. "Well, thank you."

Fidelma went to turn to get back on her horse when a thought stopped her. "Pat can I ask you something?"

Pat simply nodded.

"Do you know the merrows?"

"That your granny married into?" asked old Pat. "I know them."

"Did you ever believe that Meara destroyed the cap?" asked Fidelma

Old Pat tutted and shook his head. "Meara would not have done such a thing; she was a sweet girl from what I knew of her."

"That's what I thought," exclaimed Fidelma

"I would be looking at that Crevan chap, I never liked him," said old Pat all of a sudden.

"Crevan?" asked Fidelma frowning, "Their brother? Why would he destroy the cap?"

"I have no idea," answered old Pat,"but, I do know that while he was King, he made some enemies and I do not think his brother Mon was ever aware of that."

Fidelma stared at old Pat, once again he had provided her with some vital information, she hesitated for a moment before bounding over and giving old Pat a brief hug, startling the old man.

"Thank you, Pat," Fidelma grinned, "once again you have been a great help."

"You're welcome young Fidelma."

Fidelma turned away and climbed back on board Dílís. "Will I see you here again Pat?"

"Oh, I doubt it," old Pat shook his head, "I'm getting too old for this now, it's time for me to pass my gift on now."

"Oh no," Fidelma's face fell, "I'm sorry to hear that."

"You won't be." Old Pat said simply as he turned away and headed back towards the forest leaving Fidelma and Dílís watching after him.

CHAPTER 19:

Fidelma arrived back at An Crann Darach Sean clearly animated from her conversation with old Pat.

"How was your ride with Dílís?" Fairy Áine asked as Fairy Eimear let Fidelma in.

"Amazing!" gushed Fidelma. "So remember old Pat whom I met when I was away with my parents?"

"The one who told you the story of the Man from the North and the Woman from the South?" asked Fairy Áine

"Yes," smiled Fidelma. "Well I now know why *you* didn't know who he was!"

The fairies all looked at Fidelma expectantly.

"His name is actually Padraig!" Fidelma exclaimed.

"The leprechauns protector?" asked Fairy Áine.

"Yes!" said Fidelma as she sat down at the table and helped herself to some tea. "So you do know him?"

"Yes yes of course," replied Fairy Áine. "Well now there is a surprise, I have not seen Padraig in an age, I doubt he is about here as often as he used to be"

"Yes, well he is quite old," explained Fidelma. "He said it's almost time for him to pass his gift on now"

"To his grandson?" Fairy Caoimhe asked as she poured tea for herself, Fairy Áine and Fairy Eimear.

Fidelma shrugged. "I'm not sure, maybe."

"He is a brave age now is Padraig." said Fairy Áine. "He started here not long after your granny!"

"Well," began Fidelma, "that's not all he had to say"

"Go on," Fairy Áine encouraged, and Fidelma repeated what old Pat had told her about his theory on the destroyed cap.

"Oh Fidelma," sighed Fairy Áine. "You said your mother was what? 48?"

Fidelma simply nodded.

"Whatever happened to the cap," said Fairy Áine. "It was a very long time ago."

"So, what are you saying?" asked Fidelma frowning. "That I should just forget about it?"

"I don't know Fidelma, who will it help now?" said Fairy Áine.

"Well, it will help Meara for a start. She could go home again, be reunited with King Mon, we cannot sit by and let her continue to be punished for something she might not have even done!" Fidelma protested.

Fairy Áine was thoughtful for a moment. "Very well so," she said eventually, "we will look into it."

Fidelma put her hand across the table and grabbed Fairy Áines hand. "Thank you Fairy Áine, I just have a feeling about this."

Fidelma drained her tea from her cup. "Can we go visit Grandad again?"

"Now?" asked Fairy Áine. "Fidelma you have been here for a while already, are you not tired?"

"Tired? No way!" exclaimed Fidelma "I'm pumped now, ready to solve this atrocity."

Fairy Áine couldn't help but smile at Fidelma's enthusiasm.

Fidelma and Fairy Áine arrived at King Mon's castle, he was not expecting them this time, so the door was opened by the cook, who once again bowed to Fidelma and Fairy Áine. She led them through to the Great Hall and told them to sit down at the table as she disappeared behind the other door.

Fidelma had just sat down when the door opened, and little Nellie bounded into the room. "Fidelma!" she squealed as she threw her arms around Fidelma. Fidelma hugged the girl tightly. "I only seen you the other day Nellie."

"Yes, but I did not know that you were coming today Fidelma, it is such a lovely surprise!"

Fidelma smiled affectionately at little Nellie. The cook appeared again with a fairy sized chair and table which she set up on the main table for Fairy Áine before disappearing again behind the door.

"Is it true that you're a merrow Fidelma?" little Nellie asked eagerly

Fidelma smiled and shook her head. "No little Nellie, I'm not really a merrow but apparently I have inherited some of their traits."

"Wow!" exclaimed little Nellie, "That must be amazing."

Fidelma shrugged "I haven't really used it since the battle with Ellén Trechend."

With that the main door to the Great Hall opened and King Mon walked in, Fidelma stood up as Mon opened up his arms towards her. "Fidelma dear, what a lovely surprise!"

Fidelma walked over and hugged him. "Hello Grandad." King Mon kissed her on her head.

He took a seat at the head of the table and cook arrived again with a tray of tea for everyone.

"So," began King Mon. "To what do I owe this pleasure, I mean, you are welcome anytime, but I have a feeling there is a reason for your visit!"

Fidelma nodded. "There is a reason Grandad, I met with someone today, his name is Padraig, he's the Protector of the Leprechauns."

King Mon nodded knowingly. "I know Padraig, I have not seen him in many years though, but I remember him as a very wise man."

"Well, that's good," said Fidelma. "It's good you remember him as being wise because today he said something to me that I don't think you're going to like!"

"Go on," encouraged King Mon.

Fidelma looked to Fairy Áine who nodded to her. "Well he also believed that Meara was not the one responsible for destroying the cap"

King Mon nodded. "Had he anyone else in mind Fidelma?"

"Yes… Crevan."

Fidelma watched King Mon as he reacted, he frowned before pushing back his chair and walking towards the window.

"Did he have anything to back up his suspicions?" he asked Fidelma without turning around.

"He said Crevan had made some enemies while he was King," said Fidelma when she was suddenly interrupted by a voice she did not recognise.

"And what use would a King be if he did not make some enemies?"

Fidelma spun around to see a man standing behind her, he looked vaguely like King Mon only less handsome.

King Mon turned around with a thunderous look on his face. "Crevan?" he shouted, making everyone jump. "I think it is time you told me the truth!"

"I have nothing to tell," announced Crevan. "Yes, I made some enemies, I thought that was what a ruler needed to do, but then, I guess that is what makes *you* the better King!"

King Mon shook his head. "When you have enemies you and your people can never sleep soundly in your beds, you are constantly under threat. I do not want this for my people, for my kingdom."

Fidelma looked at her grandad with pride, he did make a great King.

Crevan simply shrugged. "Like I said, this is what makes you the better king."

"You know we brought little Nellie here because we said it was the safest place for her, because we have no enemies, no battles." Argued King Mon.

"And so we don't," answered Crevan. "Little Nellie *is* safe here, the enemies that I had are no longer our enemies, I sorted it."

"Sorted it how?" asked King Mon.

Crevan now laughed nervously. "Come on Mon, what is this? I have not been King for many many years, what does it matter now?"

"Did you destroy the cap?" King Mon asked his brother.

"Meara destroyed the cap," replied Crevan annoyed now. "I told you that."

"And that is what concerns me Crevan," said King Mon and the two brothers glared at each other.

Fairy Áine stood up. "Maybe we should go now," she said, looking from King Mon to Fidelma, "we can come back tomorrow?"

"Yes," nodded King Mon. "I think that would be wise, Crevan and I have a lot to talk about."

CHAPTER 20:

It was Saturday afternoon and was shaping up to be a dry day at least, so Fidelma decided to go for a walk as far as the library, she had some books she needed to return. She was sitting on the end of the stairs tying the laces on her runners when her brother Sean came in through the front door.

"Aaron said to call in for him if you're heading out Fidelma," he said to his sister as he hung his jacket up.

"Were you talking to Aaron?" Fidelma asked.

"Yeah, I went to his match," shrugged Sean. "He played well, scored two points."

"Very good," replied Fidelma. "Did they win?"

"They did," said Sean. "They won by a point, against St. Vincents."

Fidelma raised her eyebrows. "Good stuff."

"Where are ye off to anyway?" Sean asked.

"Just to the library." Fidelma indicated the three books sitting on the hall table. "Have to leave those back."

"Exciting stuff," mocked Sean as he hit Fidelma playfully and headed on up the stairs.

Fidelma grabbed her jacket and headed out the front door and turned up Aaron's driveway, ringing the doorbell when she got there.

Mrs. Murphy opened the door. "Ah Fidelma, how are ye?"

"I'm good thanks Mrs Murphy, is he about?"

"He just jumped into the shower Fidelma after his match, but he won't be long, come on in and wait for him."

Fidelma went into the house that sometimes felt like a second home to her she had spent that much time in it over the years, herself and Aaron had grown up together, she was only nine months older than him, so they were always together.

Fidelma had followed Mrs Murphy into the kitchen where she was doing her ironing with the radio on in the background.

"Will ye have a cup of tea luv?" she asked Fidelma.

"Ah I won't thanks Mrs. Murphy, maybe when we come back from the library."

"Aren't yis gas," laughed Mrs. Murphy, "yourself and Aaron must be the only young people who still use the library!"

"Oh, you'd be surprised," said Fidelma. "Lots of ones still use the library, you should join it yourself, you love those crime novels don't you?"

"Oh, I do love a good crime novel Fidelma, do they have those at the library?"

"Ah Mrs Murphy, they have every genre of book, you'd get all the crime novels you could read there!"

"Ah I didn't even realise," said Mrs Murphy. "Sure all our Aaron gets from it are Irish history books, between that and the DVD's he buys online, he's obsessed!"

Fidelma stifled a giggle, Mrs Murphy was not exaggerating, Aaron did love Irish history. Aaron walked into the kitchen just then in a burst of Lynx body spray.

"Howaye Fidelma," he greeted her. "What's the plan?"

"I need to take these books back to the library, have you any to return?" she asked.

"No, I'm still reading that one I got last time, it's great Fidelma it goes right back, all about the Fianna and all…but I'll walk with ye, come on."

"Bye Mrs. Murphy!"

"See ye later Mam!"

"Bye kids," Mrs. Murphy shouted after them, "be good."

"So, you're enjoying that book then?" Fidelma asked Aaron as they walked along companionably.

"Fascinating Fidelma," gushed Aaron. "Fionn mac Cumhail was some boy though, do you know that some people don't even believe those stories?"

"Do you believe them?" Fidelma asked

"Yeah, it's part of our history Fidelma, it's in our blood, ye know? We could be descendants of some of the Fianna for all we know, I think that's fascinating, you probably think I'm mad?"

"No," said Fidelma. "I'm with you on this one Aaron, I've gotten into all those stories now too."

Aaron put his arm around Fidelma. "That's what makes us such a good match!" He plonked an awkward kiss on her cheek as they walked.

"Some of the fianna were only our age when they took part in battles Fidelma, could you imagine that?" Aaron asked thoughtfully.

Fidelma grinned. "Yeah, I think I probably could."

"Do you think you'd be able for it Fidelma, if you had to battle it out for your family or your kingdom or something?"

"Oh absolutely," said Fidelma. "You'd be surprised what I'm capable of when it comes to it!"

Fidelma was back in An Crann Darach Sean.

"So," began Fairy Áine. "King Mon has sent for us Fidelma, he asked for us to head straight to his kingdom when you arrived."

"Oh, sounds ominous," replied Fidelma. "Is everything alright?"

"Well, he didn't say...the note just contained the request for our visit."

"Ok well we'll get going then, shall we?" and Fidelma headed towards the door.

"I've prepared Dílís for you both," called Fairy Caoimhe as they headed out the door.

The two friends made their way across the field towards Dílís, who, as always was pleased to see Fidelma.

Fidelma patted her horse fondly and herself and Fairy Áine climbed aboard.

"Just to the Killarney portal Dílís," said Fidelma.

"Yes, Fairy Caoimhe said that, is everything alright Fidelma?"

"Well yes, I think so," said Fidelma. "I mean we don't really know but we hope so."

It wasn't long before they arrived at the cave and Fidelma and Fairy Áine climbed down, scattering some oats on the ground for Dílís as they did.

"Be careful!"

"Always!" Fidelma assured her horse.

The girls arrived on the other side of the cave greeted by Cook. "Oh, thank goodness you are both here" she said.

"What's wrong?" Fidelma asked, placing her hand on Cooks arm.

"I am worried about King Mon, he had a thunderous row with Crevan last night, he has been pacing the floor all day and has hardly eaten anything."

Fidelma and Fairy Áine exchanged looks. "Alright," said Fidelma in a comforting tone, "lets go up to the castle and we will see how we can help."

The three of them made their way back up to the entrance of the castle and into the great hall where King Mon was standing staring out the window. Fidelma turned to Cook. "Where is little Nellie?"

"She is at a friends house today." Cook told a relieved Fidelma.

Fidelma simply nodded. "Ok thank you, could you maybe prepare us some tea please? And some food for King Mon?"

Cook bowed to Fidelma and made her way out of the Great Hall. Fidelma looked at Fairy Áine who encouraged her to approach the King.

Fidelma walked over and gently touched King Mon on his arm, "Grandad?"

King Mon turned around with tears in his eyes, Fidelma searched his face for answers but all she could see was anguish.

"Tell me what happened." Fidelma said and gently led King Mon towards his seat at the table.

"Last night I begged Crevan to tell me the truth- ," he began, "-and nothing could have prepared me for what he said"

Fidelma waited for her grandad to continue.

"All the time he was King, he made so many enemies, hatched so many disastrous plans and got into so many fights, all without me knowing."

"Well, you weren't here," offered Fidelma.

King Mon shook his head. "I was here for six months at a time

Fidelma and I never suspected anything, I was too wrapped up in my own life, my love for your grandmother and my children whilst Crevan put our kingdom, our people at risk, again and again.

Fidelma reached out to take King Mon's hand, she felt sorry for him. "But that's ok Grandad, you weren't the king, it wasn't your job, it was Crevans job, he is the one who failed."

"That may be so," said King Mon sadly, "but I was the one who banished my own sister, my dear sweet Meara." Fidelma watched as a tear slid down his face.

"Tell me what happened Grandad." Fidelma gently prompted.

King Mon sucked in a deep breath before speaking. "The Muckie!"

Fairy Áine gasped. Fidelma looked from the fairy to her Grandad, "What's the Muckie?" she asked.

"A Monster Fidelma," said Fairy Áine, shaking her head before addressing the King, "What has the Muckie got to do with all of this King Mon?"

"Crevan made an enemy of the Muckie while he was King, he tried to take over Lake Muckross which is ruled by the Muckie."

"How dangerous is this Muckie?" Fidelma cut in.

"Extremely dangerous Fidelma," said Fairy Áine. "She really is a Monster, she is like a dragon who lives under the water, she's covered with hundreds of sharp spines similar to hedgehogs' quills except these are huge, the size of spears and twice as sharp, when she attacks these shoot out and can easily kill."

Fidelma raised her eyebrows, for once lost for words so King Mon continued.

"The Muckie threatened our kingdom, she threatened to kill everyone in it unless Crevan surrendered to her."

"Surrendered to her how?" asked Fairy Áine.

"She wanted Crevan to give up the crown, but Crevan tried to trick her into believing he had given it up when I had come back for my six months, but the Muckie was not to be fooled, she was angered and ordered Crevan to both give up the crown and." King Mon stopped here and broke down in tears, Fidelma rushed to his side

"Oh Grandad," she soothed. "What is it, what happened?"

Between sobs King Mon continued. "She ordered Crevan to give her Meara as her prisoner in exchange for allowing him to keep his life."

Fidelma's hands flew to her mouth "Meara is being kept prisoner by that Monster?"

King Mon nodded through his tears.

"All this time." Muttered Fairy Áine shaking her head in disbelief.

Fidelma stood up suddenly. "We need to rescue her!" she exclaimed.

"I know," said King Mon, "but how? I do not have an army!"

Fidelma nodded. "No, but we know someone who does!"

CHAPTER 21:

They were in An Crann Darach Sean, Fairy Áine had sent for Cailte Mac Ronaín and they were awaiting his arrival. Fairies Eimear and Caoimhe were getting the tea and some brown bread. Fairies Fennan, Pirkko and Gittan were preparing theirs and Fidelma's weapons. They had learned a lot from their battle with Balor and the formorians, so they were busy making silín paste to dip the arrows into.

The tea had just been set on the table when Cailte entered, Fairy Áine stood up and embraced him. "Thank you for coming at such short notice."

"Anything for the Queen." he smiled.

Fidelma stood up from the table now. "Cailte I'm afraid we need your help again, and possibly the help of the Fianna."

"That is no problem Fidelma, who are we battling with this time?"

"The Muckie," said Fairy Áine.

Cailte turned to look at the fairy "As in, the Monster that lives in Muckross lake?"

"That's the one," said Fidelma. "What do you think?"

Cailte rubbed at his jaw. "I think we will definitely need the Fianna."

"Sit and have some tea with us," said Fairy Áine, "and we will tell you the story."

Cailte took a seat at the table and Fairy Áine sat beside him as Fidelma began the tale of Crevan and the Muckie.

Cailte shook his head in disbelief. "So after all this time poor Meara is being held captive?"

"I'm afraid so," said Fidelma

"Do we know if she's even still alive?" asked Cailte.

"Crevan seems to think so," said Fidelma, "although it's hard to believe a word that comes out of his mouth now."

Cailte nodded thoughtfully. "We will need to fight her from the shore, I cannot see anyway else." Cailte looked around him but nobody contradicted him so he continued. "So we will have to coax her out of the water somehow."

"I can do that!" Fidelma spoke up, everyone looked at her concerned, "well I can breathe under water remember?"

Fairy Áine shook her head. "Fidelma it will be incredibly dangerous!"

"Yes," said Fidelma simply. "Of course it will be dangerous, but come on Fairy Áine, I am the protector, a true warrior you said."

"I know," said Fairy Áine, "and believe me it's not that I don't have faith in you, it's just that you mean so much to us Fidelma, we got such a fright when Ellén Trechend took you that time"

Fidelma cut Fairy Áine off. "I know Fairy Áine, but I will be fine, I promise."

Cailte Mac Ronaín spoke again. "What about the merrows? Can they add to our army?"

Fidelma shook her head. "No, they're peaceful, they don't really have anyone who could fight."

Cailte sighed. "Right well we better come up with a good plan so."

Suddenly a letter arrived, An Crann Darach Sean had what looked like a small fireplace which was actually a mail chute, birds or owls were generally used to send the messages.

Fairy Eimear got up to see who the letter was from, everyone watched as she picked it up and opened it, "It's from King Mon!" she announced.

Fidelma jumped up from her seat and over to Fairy Eimear who handed the letter to her, Fidelma scanned it quickly. "He says Crevan wants to help our army, Grandad has told him we don't want his help and has banished him to the Upper Lake."

"Where he banished Meara to," said Fairy Caoimhe quietly.

"Where he thought he banished her," corrected Fidelma.

There was silence for a moment before Fairy Áine spoke up. "Right, Meara is the one who matters here, so forget about Crevan."

"Yes," said Cailte, "and remember that man cannot be trusted."

"So can we agree that I will coax the Muckie out from the water?" Fidelma looked around her at everyone nodding so she continued. "What about freeing Meara? Take the Muckie down first and then free her? Or try to free Meara while we're fighting the Muckie?"

Cailte Mac Ronaín shook his head. "No Fidelma the Muckie is far too dangerous, we take her down first and then we can free Meara when it's safe to do so."

"So, we just set up on the lakeside and wait for the Muckie?" asked Fennan. "Then just start firing at her?"

"I don't think it's going to be that easy." Cailte said.

"Nobody who has taken the Muckie on has lived to tell the tale," said Fairy Áine.

"And we shouldn't underestimate her enormous size," warned Cailte Mac Ronaín, "She is absolutely gigantic, unlike anything most of us will have ever seen." Cailte paused to look around him, "and then there are her quills, if you can imagine the size of the Muckie then please try to picture the size of those deadly spines, they could kill a man in an instant, this is likely to be our toughest battle yet."

There was silence as everyone was lost in their own thoughts, then Cailte stood up. "I will go and round up the Fianna."

Fairy Áine stood up and escorted Cailte out.

CHAPTER 22:

Fidelma called into Aaron, she was wearing her tracksuit and runners, this evening when she went back to An Crann Darach Sean she would be heading into battle with a dangerous lake Monster, she wanted to make sure she was fit for it.

Aaron opened the door just as Fidelma was about to knock, he was wearing shorts and a hoodie, he looked at Fidelma standing in front of him and pulled the earphones out of his ears. "I'm going training Fidelma."

"I know," said Fidelma. "I was hoping I could come with you, do a workout?"

Aaron frowned. "I mean, you can if you want, but do you think you'll be able for it?"

Fidelma rolled her eyes. "Of course I'll be fit for it Aaron."

"Sorry," Aaron looked contrite. "I didn't mean anything by it, come on so."

The pair headed off running down towards their local park where they done a couple of laps before doing some exercises on the grass.

When they were finished, they sat on a bench drinking from their water bottles.

"Fair play Fidelma," Aaron broke the silence. "That's the GAA training we do, bit surprised how well you kept up if I'm honest."

"You'd be surprised what I'm capable of Aaron."

Fidelma arrived at An Crann Darach Sean that evening, she was feeling a little bit apprehensive but also highly charged. The Oak Tree was a hive of activity with fairies scurrying about, preparing for the battle.

Not long after Fidelma arrived, Cailte appeared followed by some of the Fianna. They began setting out their plan, Fidelma was to go under the lake and antagonize the Muckie which would hopefully draw her to the surface.

"As soon as she comes to the surface she will engage in battle," warned Cailte. "The Muckie loves to battle because she always wins."

"Fidelma come outside with me, there is something I want to show you."

Fidelma stood up and followed Cailte outside, stopping in shock at what she saw behind the tree. The only way Fidelma could describe it, was a giant bird, but not like Aoife, this one was pure white and didn't look evil; its feathers glistened in the sun, it was magnificent.

"This is Énna," said Cailte. "She belongs to my uncle."

Fidelma looked at Cailte "Fionn Mc Cumhaill?"

Cailte simply nodded, "he said we could borrow her; I think she will be a vital ally in this battle."

"It is a pleasure to meet you Fidelma!"

Fidelma touched the feathers on the birds back and stroked them, "Pleasure to meet you too Énna," she said before turning back to Cailte. "Who will ride her?"

"I will," replied Cailte. "I have experience with her," Cailte put his hand on Fidelma's arm guiding her back towards the entrance of An Crann Darach Sean. Fairy Caoimhe came out to let them back in. "We need to be able to attack from above Fidelma, it's the only way we have a chance of winning this battle."

"You make it sound like we don't have a great chance of winning Cailte."

Cailte stopped and looked at Fidelma, he sighed, "Fidelma this will not be a walk in the park that's for sure, the Muckie is absolutely enormous, as for her quills." He shook his head. "This will be our most dangerous battle yet."

Cailte turned and walked on inside, leaving Fidelma standing feeling suddenly overwhelmed. Fairy Áine noticed Fidelma and walked over to her.

"Are you alright Fidelma?" she asked.

Fidelma straightened up and nodded. "Yes Fairy Áine I'm fine thank you, I just had a moment."

Cailte was standing in the centre of the room as he addressed everyone. "There is a portal that can take us close to the shore of Muckross Lake, we will head there on horseback, I will take Énna. Everyone should have double the number of weapons we used for the battle with the formorians and make sure they're dipped in the silín, as deadly as that stuff is, it is going to take a huge amount of it to take down the Muckie."

Cailte began pacing the floor. "Fidelma will go down first and demand that the Muckie free Meara, she won't of course but Fidelma can make some threats then to lure her up for the battle."

He stopped pacing and turned to look around the room. "This is a dangerous battle but another very important one. Meara has been held prisoner for near on fifty years now, it is horrendous to think that she has been there that long, we need to free her, and taking down the Muckie is the only way to do it."

"Now," Cailte continued. "Crevan has asked that he be allowed join us in battle, but I do not feel he can be trusted so please let me know if you see him around the lake. Alright, are we ready?"

The Fianna men all raised their weapons and roared. The fairies and Fidelma all gave each other high fives and then one of the fairies opened the door and they all filed out.

CHAPTER 23:

The troop arrived on the shore of Muckross lake, as they approached, they noticed something in the water. Cailte and Fidelma rode closer to look and Fidelma realised soon enough that it was Crevan in the water.

Fidelma got down from her horse and walked over to the water's edge. "Crevan what are you doing here?" she called.

Crevan swam closer to the shore. "Fidelma I am truly sorry for what I have done, please forgive me, please let me help rescue Meara, let me make amends."

Fidelma looked at Crevan, he looked heartbroken, she almost felt sorry for him but then she remembered everything he had done, taking her grandfather away from his family and her resolve hardened.

"I do not doubt that you are sorry now Crevan," Fidelma called to him. "But I cannot let you have any part in this, you need to leave now, go to the Upper Lake where my grandad banished you."

Crevan nodded solemnly to Fidelma and then disappeared beneath the murky water.

Cailte rode over beside Fidelma. "Let us hope that is the last we see of him"

Fidelma just nodded, then she climbed down from Dílís. "I'm ready to go now Cailte, no point in putting this off."

"Fidelma, you have had no time to prepare, are you sure you can do this?" Cailte asked.

"I think I'm better off just going for it Cailte," Fidelma said. "I know

now that my gills will kick in, once that happens, I'll be fine."

Cailte put his hand on Fidelma's shoulder. "Take care."

Fidelma smiled in reply before taking off her shoes and then her hoody and tracksuit bottoms, she was wearing a swimsuit underneath, she folded her clothes and put them into her satchel across Dílís along with her runners.

"*Fidelma I will be awaiting your return,*" her faithful horse began. "*Please do not put yourself in any unnecessary danger.*"

Fidelma put her arms around the horse's neck and hugged him tight. "Thank you Dílís, I'll see you soon."

And with that she walked into the lake, wincing as the cold water came up her legs, when it reached her tummy, she stopped for a moment to catch her breath. Fairy Áine was flying beside her, "I have every faith in you Fidelma but please be careful, you have not had time to perfect this gift."

Fidelma could only give Fairy Áine an encouraging smile, it was taking her a lot of effort to adjust to the cold water and regulate her breathing. When the water reached her shoulder, Fidelma took a deep gulp of air and went under.

Down she went, the water was so murky she could hardly see, it was dark and scary beneath the lake. Suddenly Fidelma could feel her chest burning as she fought the urge to breathe in, she felt as if she was about to pass out when all of a sudden, she felt a stinging sensation in her neck as her gills appeared and before she knew it, she was breathing underwater. It was extraordinary, Fidelma was not a strong swimmer before but now she felt as if she were a merrow, she was gliding seamlessly through the water.

She continued downwards; she knew that at the bottom of the lake was where the Muckie lay. It was getting harder to see now, the water was murky with weeds and dirt but all of a sudden Fidelma spotted the Monster, her presence was unmistakable. Cailte had warned of the Muckies size but still Fidelma was stunned and a little bit frightened by what she saw in front of her.

The Muckies quills were easily the same length of Fidelma's legs, Cailte was right, this would be a dangerous battle.

The Monster seemed to sense she had company as her sleeping eyes shot open, her eyes were as large as Fidelma's head such was her size. She spotted Fidelma straight away and bared her razor-sharp teeth. "What business have you in my lake?" she roared.

"I have come to free Meara!" Fidelma called.

The Monster roared laughing, an evil high-pitched cackle that made Fidelma put her hands over her ears.

"Meara was given to me to in exchange for Crevan keeping his life, she is my prisoner now, unless you are here to bring me Crevan?"

"I wish no harm on Meara or Crevan, I am here to take Meara home!"

"Well then you are more foolish than you look cailín!" sneered the Monster as she began to rise from where she was lying, as she did so, Fidelma could see a cage behind her where Meara was lying, Fidelma hoped she was still alive.

"It is not just me!" Fidelma called quickly. "I have an army with me on the shore above, we have all come to take Meara home."

The Monsster laughed again "The only thing they will be taking home is your lifeless body" and with that she lifted one of her paws so quick that Fidelma hardly had time to react, the Monster tried to step on Fidelma but just managed to trap her foot, Fidelma wriggled in agony trying to get free when all of a sudden a dagger was pierced straight into the paw of the enormous Monster causing it to lift its paw in pain and allowing Fidelma swim away. As she turned around to see who was yielding the dagger Fidelma was shocked to see Crevan.

"Quick Fidelma!" he called. "Go to the surface, fight your battle, I will free Meara!"

Fidelma hesitated for a second before making a bee line for the surface, she swam at full speed conscious that the Muckie would not be far behind her.

On the shore the team watched with bated breath, scanning the water for any movement when Cailte suddenly pointed to the centre of the lake. "Over there!" he shouted.

They watched as Fidelma broke through the waters surface, she shot up about five metres in the air like a dolphin before landing back gracefully in the lake. Fidelma put her hand up and waved "Get ready!" she roared. "She's coming" and she swam as fast as she could to the shore towards Dílís. She got out of the water and quickly grabbed her clothes and put them on when she heard what sounded like the rumble of thunder, but it turned out to be the arrival of the Muckie.

"Places everyone!" Fidelma roared.

Cailte was about to take off when Fidelma called to him "Crevan is here!"

"What?" Cailte was dumbfounded.

"He saved my life!" she called. "He went back for Meara; we need to take down this Monster!"

Cailte nodded briefly before taking to the sky, Fidelma jumped onto Dílís and prepared her bow and arrows just as the still water broke and the Muckie emerged in a thunderous roar.

Everyone began letting off their arrows in the direction of the Monster, but Fidelma quickly realised their arrows were so small in comparison to the Muckie, they were having very little effect.

Cailte was above the Muckie now and was also firing arrows, but Fidelma realised the only way they were going to take her down was with the Fianna's spears and the only way the Fianna would get close enough was if she came onto the land.

"Fall back!" Fidelma called. "We need her on the land!"

Dílís began retreating away from the lake when suddenly the Monster shot out about twenty of her quills in one go, one just narrowly missed Fidelma and Dílís, landing in the sand beside them Fidelma shivered at how deadly it looked. Still, they retreated away from the lake, their plan was working, the Muckie was following them. Another twenty or so quills were released and Fidelma heard a roar from behind her, it was one of the Fianna, he had been struck, but they had to keep going. Fidelma watched on as Cailte swooped down on Énnas back, as close to the Monster as he dared and with great force, threw a spear towards the Monster, connecting with the back of its neck, the Muckie let out an agonizing roar, but it was not enough to take her down, she shot out another bunch of quills and another roar came from the Fianna.

Fidelma began firing off a succession of arrows, aiming for the Monsters' head, knowing her aim was spot on and hoping the poison would begin to take effect.

As the Muckie made its way onto land the Fianna changed position and galloped towards the Monster, their spears and shields raised, the fairies flying over head firing off their tiny but poisonous arrows when Fidelma spotted something in the lake, it was Crevan.

Fidelma watched as Crevan swam awkwardly towards the rocks with one arm around Meara who seemed to be semi-conscious. He helped Meara up onto the rocks before pulling himself up beside her as Fidelma looked on with relief and contentment that Crevan had come good in the end.

Fidelma turned to see Cailte swoop down again and throw another spear into the Monster, catching her in her lower back but this time as she cried out, she lifted her enormous tail and swiped at Énna and Cailte knocking them out of the sky and sending them hurtling towards the ground, she heard Fairy Áine scream at the sight.

The Fianna were close to the Monster now, so Fidelma took off in that direction too and began shooting off more arrows, aiming for the face, she watched as the Fianna made contact with the Muckie, ramming their spears deep into her she let out the loudest most piercing roar, shooting out about fifty of her quills as she fell heavily to the ground. The Fianna protected themselves with their shields from the falling quills, Dílís roared at Fidelma.

"Watch out!" she ducked her head against Dílís' neck before crying out in pain as a quill made contact with her leg.

Fidelma quickly looked up in time to see the last of the quills falling, she watched as one fell where Crevan and Meara were sheltering on the rocks, she called out, "Crevan! Meara! Watch out!" but it was too late, one of the quills landed straight through Crevan's heart killing him instantly.

Fidelma watched helplessly as Meara cried out in anguish. Fidelma felt her eyes fill with emotion, Crevan had risked his life for her and after all these years, lost his life saving Meara. Fidelma looked around her, there were a few men lying wounded and at least two looked like they had lost their lives, she watched as the fairies re grouped and was relieved to see they were all accounted for except for Fairy Áine but she could see her flying over to where Cailte and Énna had come down.

"Fidelma are you ok? Talk to me?"

Fidelma patted Dílís on his neck. "I think I'm ok thanks Dílís, I'm hit but its not bad, I'm worried for Cailte though can you take me to where he fell, please?"

"What about Meara?" Dílís asked.

"I know Dílís, but she is safe, I just need to know that Cailte is alive, please?"

"Your wish is my command Fidelma," and Dílís began to take off in the direction of where Cailte went down.

As they got closer Fidelma seen Fairy Áine landing beside Cailte and Énna, she looked distraught. Fidelma jumped down off Dílís and ran over "Is he alright?" she called out.

"I don't know, I don't know!" shouted a panicked Fairy Áine, "I don't think he's breathing!"

Fidelma got down on her knees and put her ear to Cailtes chest, nothing. Fidelma muttered a swear word under her breath, she had done CPR training at the local community centre with Aaron last year, but it was one of those things you hoped you never had to use, she looked at Fairy Áine who was frantic with worry. Fidelma bent her head again to check for breathing but there was nothing, she positioned her hands on the centre of Cailtes chest and began to push hard and fast, she could hear Fairy Áine crying out.

"Fidelma what are you doing? What's happening?" but Fidelma had to just block her out so she could concentrate on what she was doing, she knew at this point, according to her training she should be calling 999 but obviously that was not an option here. After she had done thirty presses Fidelma stopped and done two rescue breaths, she waited, still nothing. She started again with the compressions, she done another thirty before doing the rescue breaths again, just as she was about to do the second breath, Cailte gasped and began coughing. Fidelma sat back on her hunkers with relief as Fairy Áine fluttered in front of Cailtes face, crying hysterically. "You're alive! I can't believe it! I thought I had lost you."

Fidelma felt herself begin to shake when she felt a tiny hand on her shoulder, it was Fennan. "Hey Fidelma," she said gently. "Are you ok?"

Tears sprung to Fidelma's eyes, she fought desperately to keep them there, but they spilled freely down her cheeks.

Fennan wiped at the tears gently. "Ssh Ssh, you're alright, you're alright, let me look at your leg Fidelma."

Fidelma shook her head as she struggled to stand up. "No thank you Fennan, I need to go see Meara." and she limped towards Dílís.

"You saved his life Fidelma!" exclaimed Dílís.

Fidelma simply nodded, biting her lip, and swallowing the lump that formed in her throat again.

They headed over towards the rocks, Fidelma took a deep shuddering breath as she watched Meara sit on the rock with Crevens head resting in her lap as she caressed his hair, crying softly.

Fidelma got down from Dílís, wincing as she briefly put weight on her leg, she limped over to Meara and sat down beside her on the rocks.

"I'm so sorry Meara," she said gently.

"He was still my brother," Meara said simply.

CHAPTER 24:

They were sitting around the table in the Great Hall with King Mon. It was a few days since the battle, and everyone was slowly recovering. King Mon of course had been devastated to hear about the death of Crevan, but he took comfort in the fact that he died saving Meara and that he saved Fidelma's life too. Nothing could change what had happened all those years ago, but it was time for healing and forgiveness.

Meara was slowly recovering for the trauma of being held prisoner by the Muckie and herself and little Nellie were fast becoming firm friends. They had lost two members of the Fianna, Fidelma felt awful, but Cailte reassured her that they knew the risk, fighting battles was their life. As for Cailte, he made a full recovery as did the beautiful Énna. Fidelma's leg was badly cut but the fairies took good care off her after the battle and when she got home, she told her parents she came off her bike.

So now Fidelma, King Mon, Meara and little Nellie were having tea and delicious Victoria Sponge.

"I cannot tell you how proud I am of you Fidelma," exclaimed King Mon.

Fidelma smiled. "Grandad you've said that a thousand times"

King Mon reached over and took Fidelma's hand, "and I will say it a thousand more," he replied, "I should have listened to your grandmother, she knew something was not right with Crevan's story, just as you knew."

Fidelma shook her head. "It was a tough one Grandad; you were torn between your brother and your sister and Crevan could be quite convincing from what I hear."

Meara turned to Fidelma. "I cannot thank you enough Fidelma, I thought I would die in that cage."

"Once I knew the truth Meara," said Fidelma. "I vowed to rescue you, it's what my granny would have done."

"Your granny was a great woman Fidelma," cried Meara. "I loved her dearly, like a sister, I could never have betrayed her."

Fidelma nodded. "I know Meara, and my granny knew that too."

Fidelma and Aaron were in the living room in Fidelma's home, they were looking up cinema times on Fidelma's laptop.

"Ok," said Fidelma. "Definitely Spiderman Homecoming? Before I click on it?"

"Definitely!" exclaimed Aaron. "Come on Fidelma click on it, tickets are selling out fast we don't want to miss out"

Fidelma giggled as she clicked and booked 2 tickets for the following evening for the new Spiderman movie. After a couple of minutes, she announced. "Ok, all done!" and she logged out and shut down the laptop.

"So, what do you want to do now?" Aaron asked.

"Don't mind." Shrugged Fidelma.

"I was gonna suggest a walk but is your leg still sore?"

"Ah it's not too bad," said Fidelma, "but it is still a bit sore."

"Wanna just chill out and watch a movie?" asked Aaron.

"Sounds perfect," smiled Fidelma grabbing the remote. "Just the one though I've something on this evening."

Aaron shook his head. "Fidelma you're very mysterious, what do you be up to in the evenings?"

Fidelma was caught off guard, she took a few seconds to answer, "Ah girlie stuff Aaron."

"Hmmm," Aaron shook his head. "I'm not buying it, one of these days I'll find out you know."

Fidelma just laughed.

CHAPTER 25:

It was later that evening and Fidelma had just arrived at An Crann Darach Sean, there was great excitement there today and everyone was busy.

"Fidelma, do you want to go get changed?" Fairy Eimear asked, "I've hung your dress up in your room for you."

"Thank you, Fairy Eimear," Fidelma gave the fairy a hug. "You're such a talent, where's Fairy Áine?"

"Fennan took her down to get ready, isn't it all so exciting?" Fairy Eimear beamed.

"Oh absolutely," and Fidelma headed off to her room to get ready. When she walked in, she seen a very pretty dress hanging up on the hook, Fairy Eimear had made it for her, she really was a fairy of many talents.

Fidelma put the dress on and ran a hairbrush through her freshly washed hair, she slipped her feet into a pair of sandals she brought with her, she wished she had a full-length mirror, but she thought she looked alright.

Fidelma made her way to the kitchen to some "oohs" and "aahhs" from the fairies.

"Do we have time for tea?" she asked, looking around at the fairies in their pretty dresses. "Wow you all look wonderful!"

"Why thank you," giggled Fairy Caoimhe curtsying. "It's been such a fun morning getting ready, sit down and I'll bring over some tea."

Fidelma sat at the table with Fairy Eimear. "You've done a great job with the dresses Fairy Eimear"

"Thank you," gushed the fairy. "Fairy Caoimhe helped me, there was so much to do but we're happy with how everything turned out!"

Fairy Eimear had just brought the tea to the table when Fairy Fennan walked in, she had a beautiful blue lace dress on, her hair hung loosely around her shoulders intertwined with bluebells, she looked beautiful.

"Please stand for your Fairy Queen!" she announced.

Fairy Eimear and Fidelma stood up from the table and the rest of the fairies all gathered around.

Fidelma watched as Fairy Áine seemed to glide into the room, she was wearing a beautiful full length cream coloured lace dress, her hair fell in loose ringlets down around her shoulders and on her head was a crown of bluebells.

Fidelma ran to her with tears in her eyes. "Oh Fairy Áine!" she exclaimed. "You look absolutely breath-taking!"

Fairy Áine beamed "Thank you Fidelma, you look lovely too!"

Fidelma put her arms around Fairy Áine and held her tightly as Fairy Áine hugged her back. "I cannot believe you're getting married!"

Fairy Áine giggled. "Me neither!"

"Well, it's about time if you ask me," laughed Fairy Fennan as she put her arms around the two of them. "Come on, we have time for a quick cup of tea before we head out." The trio walked over and sat down at the table."Now," continued Fairy Fennan, "when we get outside, I am going to use my magic to make Fairy Áine human sized."

Fairy Áine nodded at this; she was familiar with the plans for the day.

"Oh wow! Really?" Fidelma exclaimed. "I've never seen you human sized!"

"We can actually do it anytime," explained Fairy Fennan. "But we rarely choose to do it, we are fairies after all but alas today is an exception," and she smiled at her sister.

Soon it was time to go, the fairies all made their way outside, Fairy Fennan made herself, Fairy Áine and Fidelma human sized and they began to make their way to where the ceremony was taking place.

Fidelma gasped in awe at what she seen, ahead of them was a beautiful wooden alter adorned with ivy and bluebells.

"Wait," said Fidelma, "is that-"

"Yes," explained Fairy Eimear, "this is the very alter we made for your grandmother and King Mon."

"It really is beautiful." Declared Fidelma, she found it a bit emotional that her grandparents had wed on the very same alter.

There were some wooden seats before the alter and most of them were already filled with some familiar faces, on the other side was a bench with tiny seats for the fairies.

Fidelma stopped and turned to Fairy Áine. "Not that you need it, but best of luck" She kissed Fairy Áine gently on the cheek. "I wish you and Cailte a lifetime of happiness."

Fairy Áine took Fidelma's hand and squeezed it gently before Fidelma went and took her seat beside her Grandad, Meara, and little Nellie.

Cailte was standing in the alter in his finest warrior outfit, he looked very handsome indeed. There were three leprechauns standing to the left of the alter, two with fiddles and one with a tin whistle, they struck up a beautiful tune and everyone turned to watch Fairy Fennan make her way forward followed by a glowing Fairy Áine.

Fidelma felt herself well up with emotion as she watched the ceremony, it was beautiful, she watched as the celebrant tied a piece of ribbon around Fairy Áine's hands and then Cailtes before bounding them together. She listened as they made their beautiful vows; "Ye are blood of my blood, and bone of my bone. I give ye my body that we two might be one, I give ye my spirit, 'till our life shall be done..." It was truly beautiful.

As the ceremony came to an end Cailte spoke. "I knew as a child that I would one day marry you Fairy Áine, and even though we went the long way around, we got here in the end, and I could not be happier."

Everyone clapped and Fairy Áine smiled her biggest smile yet. Fidelma was so happy for her two friends.

Once the ceremony was over, they made their way back to An Crann Darach Sean where everyone was made fairy size to go inside for the party. There was music, dancing, and food. Fidelma had so much fun but eventually she had to ask Fairy Áine to take her home.

As Fidelma arrived back in her bedroom she turned to say goodnight to Fairy Áine. "Goodnight my dear friend, I hope you've enjoyed your wonderful day, I am so happy for you and for Cailte, he loves you very much you know?"

Fairy Áine nodded. "I do know Fidelma, and I love him too," she flew up and kissed Fidelma on her forehead. "Goodnight my dearest friend and thank you so much for everything, enjoy Aaron's birthday tomorrow."

And with that she was gone. Fidelma yawned, she was absolutely exhausted as she pulled on her pyjamas, she could hardly keep her eyes open, she climbed into bed and fell asleep straight away.

Epilogue:

It was the day of Aaron's birthday, Fidelma was wrapping his presents, she got him a book about Irish Mythology she knew he would love and a new Dublin Jersey. She was making him his card because she couldn't find any in the shops that she was happy with. Fidelma had spoken to him on the phone earlier when he was on his way to a match, now he was having an early dinner with his family before they headed off to the cinema and then for some food afterwards. Fidelma was really looking forward to it.

Mrs. Doyle walked into the kitchen. "I heard Aaron won his match this morning Fidelma!"

"Ah yeah he was delighted," said Fidelma. "I'm going to go into him in a few minutes, he just text there to say they were finished dinner and to call in for some tea and cake."

"Ah that's nice," Mrs Doyle kissed her daughters head. "Enjoy the evening Fidelma."

Fidelma smiled up at her mother before gathering up the presents and card and heading on into Aarons.

She rang the bell and waited a moment before Mrs. Murphy opened the door.

"Ah there you are Fidelma!" she exclaimed "You're just in time for some cake, come on in."

"Thanks Mrs. Murphy," said Fidelma as she stepped into the house.

Fidelma followed Mrs. Murphy into the kitchen where she was greeted enthusiastically by Aaron, he put his arms around her and kissed her on the cheek. "Hi!"

"Happy birthday!" Fidelma handed her gifts over to Aaron.

"Aw thanks Fidelma," he said before calling over his shoulder. "Grandad come on over and meet my girlfriend, Fidelma."

Fidelma smiled and looked over Aaron's shoulder to where his grandad was chatting to Mr. Murphy, as he turned around Fidelma almost passed out in shock as the man walking towards them was old Pat.

The End

A Note from the Author

I cannot thank you enough for reading my books, you will never know how much it means to me, if you enjoyed them, please leave a review on Amazon or on my social media.

I am a sucker for Irish mythology and loved bringing it into my books. That Ireland is a magical land is not fiction, look around you in the fields to see if you can spot any Fairy Forts, watch out for ancient monuments in your travels.

Some mythological sites worth visiting in Irealnd are;

- *Newgrange*
- *The hill of Slane*
- *Loughcrew*
- *Navan Fort*
- *Beagmore Stones*
- *An Grianan Ailigh*
- *Carrowmore*
- *Carrowkeel*
- *The Rock of Cashel*

Thank you again for your support and I look forward to bringing you my next set of books! But in the meantime, stay safe and be happy!

Jennifer M Beagon

I Believe in Fairies

AFTERWORD

Although this might be the end of The Protector Trilogy it is certainly not the last you will hear of Fidelma. I am in the process of writing the next series of books and if you have read this book to the end before reading this then I am sure you know who the main character will be! So keep a watch out for them.

Don't forget you can follow me on Facebook, Instragam and now also on TikTok. If you enjoyed my books please feel free to leave a review on Amazon or via my social media.

THANK YOU AGAIN, JENNIFER M BEAGON.

Printed in Great Britain
by Amazon

83988042R00071